The Simple Case of Susan

The Simple Case of Susan

Jacques Futrelle

MINT EDITIONS

The Simple Case of Susan was first published in 1908.

This edition published by Mint Editions 2021.

ISBN 9781513224954 | E-ISBN 9781513223353

Published by Mint Editions®

 MINT
EDITIONS
minteditionbooks.com

Publishing Director: Jennifer Newens
Design & Production: Rachel Lopez Metzger
Project Manager: Micaela Clark
Typesetting: Westchester Publishing Services

To Her
All by Herself

Scituate, 1908

Contents

I

Susan's eyes were blue wells of promises unfulfilled; Susan's mouth was a scarlet bow of hope unattainable; Susan's hair was an alluring trap, baited with sunlight; Susan's nose was *retroussé*. Susan was the ever-receding rainbow, the mocking will-o'-the-wisp, intangible as the golden mist of dawn, irrepressible as the perfume of a rose, irresistible as the song of the siren. She was unexpectedness in person, a quirk in the accepted order of things, elusive as fame, fleeting as moonbeams.

Susan had a larger collection of unhappy hearts pinned up in the specimen cabinet of her affections than any other woman in her set. Even her enemies admitted this, adding thereto some spiteful, venomous thing which was intended to blunt the point—but didn't. Not that she had escaped unscathed when the city of Eros fell, for she had not. She had been seized upon by a giant among the pygmies, and lashed to the chariot wheel of matrimony. Instantly she became a demure, sedate wife, enslaving as she was enslaved, adoring as she was adored.

But it were damming the waters of Lethe to effectually repress the charm, the effervescence, the Susanism of Susan. She was still adorable from the tips of her boots to the last riotous strands of her head. There was an indisputable unanimity of masculine opinion on this last point. And her whims and caprices were still the only laws she recognized save when the master spoke, and she bowed in grateful submission.

This was Susan. Perhaps the stately Mrs. Wetmore described her more tersely when she said she was featherheaded. Be that as it may, Susan was Susan—irrevocably, everlastingly, and eternally Susan.

II

S usan was thoughtfully nibbling a *biscuit tortoni* in one corner of a Broadway confectionery shop, when the door opened and—enter a young man. He was tall and straight and clean-cut; a personal compliment to his tailor and hatter and bootmaker. There was a glowing tan on his cheeks, pleasant lines about his mouth, and the languor of idleness in his eyes. Susan glanced around inquiringly.

"Why, Dan Wilbur!" she exclaimed.

The young man turned with quick interest.

"Sue Courtenay!"

It was almost enthusiasm. He reached the table in three strides, and two strong hands closed over one delicately gloved one.

"Not Courtenay, now, Dan," Susan corrected. "Mrs. Lieutenant Paul Abercrombie Harwell Rowland, if you please."

She sat up primly under the burden of that imposing name and withdrew the gloved hand. Mr. Wilbur reluctantly allowed it to flutter away, then sat down on the opposite side of the table with mingled inquiry and surprise on his face.

"All that?" he asked. "Since when?"

"Oh, for more than two years! Hadn't you heard?"

"But what became of Charlie Beckwith?"

"Oh, he's married!" Susan smiled charmingly.

"But you were engaged to—"

"Do try one of these *biscuits*, Dan. They're delicious."

"And then there was Julian Blackwell?"

Susan shrugged her shoulders.

"And Frank Camp?"

Susan merely nibbled.

"And Ed Rainey?" he went on accusingly.

"Oh, please, Dan, don't call the roll like that," Susan pleaded. "It isn't nice, really. Some of them are married and seem to be glad of it, and the others are not married, and they seem to be equally glad of it."

"And, please, who is this Lieutenant—er—er? Would you mind saying it all over again?"

"Lieutenant Paul Abercrombie Harwell Rowland."

"Phew! Well, who *is* he?"

"Oh, you never met him," Susan assured him. "Society has been initiated into the army since you went away. But he's the dearest, darlingest—"

"Yes, of course. But after that?"

"Well, he's an army officer. He happened along after you went away three years ago and—and just married me."

Mr. Wilbur was leaning forward on the table thoughtfully stroking his chin. There was almost an incredulous expression in the listless eyes.

"An army officer," he repeated. "Well, would you mind telling me how—why did—say, how did he do it?"

"Oh, I don't know quite," Susan explained serenely. "He asked me to marry him, and I said No, and he asked me again, and I said No, and he asked me *again*, and I said No. And then he just went ahead and married me, anyway."

Mr. Wilbur smiled.

"I suppose that's the only way it could ever have been done—by main strength," he remarked after a while. "But you didn't deserve any better, Sue. I'm glad he did it."

"So am I."

A smile flickered about Susan's lips, and from the bottomless blue eyes came a flash which set Mr. Wilbur's well-ordered nerves a-tingling. He drew a long breath.

"Married!" he remarked at last. "Well, by George!"

Susan regarded him severely, with a haughty uplifting of her brows, and a prim expression about the scarlet mouth. Of course it was all right for him to be surprised—she had expected him, even wanted him to be surprised—but not *so* surprised. Why it was—it was almost insulting.

"And where have you been for three years?" Susan queried at last dutifully.

"Everywhere, almost," Mr. Wilbur replied. "Around the world once, just knocking about, and now I'm about to start on another lap. I came in yesterday from Liverpool, and this afternoon I'm starting for San Francisco to catch a steamer for the Philippines. I'm to join the Mortons at Manila for a cruise in the Sea of Japan, and later through Suez to the Mediterranean."

"This afternoon? All sudden like that?" Susan demanded. "Can't you stay over a few days?" She simply had to ask that because Dan really was a nice chap, you know.

"Oh, I don't think so," said Mr. Wilbur. "It's rather purposeless hanging around New York, and traveling is something to do, you know."

He paused and stared straight into Susan's blue eyes. "Married! By George!"

Susan favored him with a frown of reproach, which was suddenly lost in a bewildering smile, and again the unfathomable depths of her eyes flashed.

"And why are you here? Who is the girl *this* time?"

Mr. Wilbur shook his head.

"No girl," he said. "I came over merely to sign some papers to close up my grandfather's estate. I'm to do that at twelve o'clock, and at three I get a train West." Mr. Wilbur gazed into eyes suddenly grown pensive. "Sue, marriage has improved you. You are even better looking than you used to be."

The shimmering head was tilted back daringly, the lids drooped for an instant, then the head came forward again, and the blue wells of pledges unfulfilled renewed their promises.

"Dan, I know it," she replied.

"And more a flirt than ever," Mr. Wilbur mused complacently. Susan's scarlet mouth twitched invitingly. "Yes, a flirt—an outrageous, unconscionable flirt!"

"No," Susan denied pleasantly.

"You were always a flirt."

"Well, of course, I won't say—I'm not a flirt *now*, anyway."

"Nature is immutable," Mr. Wilbur went on accusingly, "therefore if you *were* a flirt you *are* a flirt."

Susan was almost on the point of smiling again, when it occurred to her that it might be injudicious, indiscreet even, in view of the expression on Mr. Wilbur's face, and she suddenly assumed a gravity portentous with meaning.

"I would be willing to stake the gloves," Mr. Wilbur continued mercilessly, "that you have led your husband a chase."

"Why, Dan, that isn't true, and it isn't fair to say such a thing," Susan denied reproachfully. "It isn't like you to be—to be—ungracious."

For an instant Mr. Wilbur awaited the illuminating smile, but her face continued serious.

"I beg your pardon," he said at last. "I didn't mean it to be as solemn as all that, really. But don't you remember that night in the Casino at Newport when—"

"Dan!"

"There never was another moon in the world like that, and—"

"Dan Wilbur!"

"And that double seat in the horseshoe where—"

"Mr. Wilbur!"

The young man leaned back in his chair and smiled into the pouting face before him. The pouting face continued serious—grew painfully so, in fact—and after a moment the under lip trembled the least bit.

"Sue, I didn't intend to hurt you," apologized Mr. Wilbur almost hastily. "I was only—"

"I'm not a—a what you said I was," she protested. "You are never to think of me that way. I am Mrs. Lieutenant—"

"—Paul—"

"—Abercrombie—"

"—Harwell—"

"—Rowland," she finished desperately. "Dan Wilbur, you make me so angry I could—could choke you, nearly. I won't have you say I'm a flirt even—"

"—if you are?"

Susan thrust a spoon viciously into the *biscuit*, and her eyes shone moistly limpid.

"That isn't what I mean at all," she protested angrily.

Mr. Wilbur suddenly relinquished his tone of banter and leaned forward again with his arms resting on the table.

"Now, let's be friends," he urged. "We may not see each other again for a long time, and we must be friends. Now, I'll have to be at my lawyer's office at noon, but I shall have finished by one o'clock. Won't you forgive me? And won't you prove your forgiveness by having luncheon with me?"

"No," Susan flashed.

"I'm going away this afternoon, and it may be for several years. Please?"

"No," Susan repeated stoutly. "I don't care if you are—I mean I'm sorry you are going away, but I won't."

One of Mr. Wilbur's hands touched the tip of her gloved finger, and she primly withdrew it.

"Is it a matter of principle?" he asked. "Is it because I have offended you? Or is it—just because?"

"It's—it's just because, Dan," and the lids fluttered down. After a moment she went on: "I'm perfectly happy, Dan—I never knew I could be so happy—and I'm the least bit afraid that Paul is the least bit jealous, and besides," she continued triumphantly, "I couldn't have luncheon with you, anyway, because—now I'll prove I'm *not* a flirt—because I'm to meet my husband at one o'clock and have luncheon with him—my husband, do you understand?"

"Your own husband!" mused Mr. Wilbur.

"My own husband," Susan repeated. "And I won't take you along, either, because after what you've said I—well, I won't take you. Really, Dan, if you weren't going away I'd almost say I hated you, but I don't really. You're a nice boy—sometimes," and a dazzling smile was his reward.

"Susan," Mr. Wilbur reproved sternly, "are you trying to flirt with me?"

"No," she stormed.

"Now, Susan?" tauntingly.

"No."

III

B ut man proposes and business interposes. So it came about that Susan's husband—Lieutenant Paul Abercrombie Harwell Rowland—did not appear to take her to luncheon. Instead, at the appointed time and place, Lieutenant Faulkner, U. S. A., arose before her with an explanation.

"Paul got a hurry call from the Army and Navy Building for a conference at one o'clock," he informed her, "and they'll probably gas all afternoon. So he sent me on to take you to chow at Sherry's. Come along."

Susan accepted the situation philosophically, and thus it came to pass that a few minutes later they were safely ensconced at a table together. The waiter took the order, then rushed away, while Lieutenant Faulkner stared silently at Susan for a time.

"Say, Sue," he inquired suddenly, "do you happen to know a Miss Stanwood—Marjorie Stanwood?"

"Marjorie Stanwood?" Susan repeated thoughtfully. "No, I don't believe I do. Why?"

"I want to meet her, and I don't know anybody who knows her," the lieutenant explained.

Susan's eyes sparkled.

"Oh, that's it?" she taunted gleefully. "Who is she?"

"She is the only daughter of a man who has so much money, he has to spend all his time dodging process-servers," Lieutenant Faulkner informed her. "Why, Sue, he's got bales of it; one of these chaps that the muckrakers pin up against the wall and do tricks with. If the sum total were written down in figures you couldn't pronounce it. *Sabe?*"

"Oh, it's the money, then?" Susan accused him.

"No. She could hang her hat on my rack if she didn't have more than—more than two or three millions to her name."

"Pretty?"

"Cleopatra's clean out of the money—a cigarette picture."

"Where did you meet her?"

"I haven't met her, that's what's the matter. I want to find somebody who knows somebody who knows somebody who knows her."

"Where did you see her, then?"

"At the opera," replied the lieutenant. "Why, Sue, she's the prettiest thing that ever lived in the world, except—except."

Susan waited confidently.

"Except whom?" she inquired.

"Except a Spanish woman who tried to stick a machete under my fifth rib during some hand-to-hand scrapping in the Philippines," replied the lieutenant reminiscently. "She was the prettiest thing that ever!"

Susan sat up haughtily.

"And, pray, what is my number on your list?" she inquired.

"Oh, of course, you beat 'em all," replied Lieutenant Faulkner absently. "But, Sue, you ought to see her."

"I have no interest whatever in her," remarked Susan coldly. "I dare say she paints, anyway."

"Well, if she does, Michael Angelo was a cartoonist."

"Or is thin and slatty looking!"

"Hebe was not in the same class."

"Or her nose is red."

"Her nose," the lieutenant rhapsodized. "Why, Sue, her nose is—is— Say, I don't know how pretty Helen of Troy was, but I'll bet if she had ever taken one look at Marjorie Stanwood she'd have hit it up cross country to the beauty specialists. And Venus? Why, she'd go hide her head in a sack."

Susan was miffed. All women are miffed when man takes occasion to remark upon the beauty of another woman. She stabbed an olive, the scarlet lips curled disdainfully, and there was an aggressive slant to her shimmering head.

"Marjorie," she remarked. "Such a messy sounding name."

"Marjorie!" repeated Lieutenant Faulkner. He pronounced it as if it were a bonbon. "I can imagine an angel named Marjorie—an angel with—"

"A red nose," Susan put in, "a thin, slatty looking angel."

Lieutenant Faulkner dropped back into his chair with an air of resignation.

"I was thinking," he observed at last, "that you might go out of your way to help a fellow meet her. Don't you remember that night when I proposed to you, and—"

"There were so many nights," Susan complained.

"Well, that last night when you turned me down hard? What did I do? Didn't I go straight and bring Paul over and introduce him to you? And didn't you marry him? Turn about is fair play. It's your time to help me. *Sabe?*"

Susan was thoughtful for a little while, and then a furtive smile grew until it utterly obliterated the wofully aggrieved expression of her face.

"I'll tell you what I'll do," she said graciously. "I'll get you a bid to the Sanger ball Thursday night, and perhaps—"

"Will she be there?" the lieutenant demanded eagerly.

"I dare say she will, if she goes anywhere, and I'll see that you are introduced, anyway."

"Sue, you're a good girl," exclaimed the lieutenant. "Tout along my game some. Tell her there wasn't anybody at Manila but me and Dewey. You perhaps don't know that I'm the most promising young man in the United States Army? Well, I am, even if the officials won't admit it. Tell that to her. One of these days I'm going to be a general, and think of the uniforms I could buy with Stanwood money? I'd look like a sunburst."

"I shall do nothing of the kind," reproved Susan. "I'll merely introduce you, and you may fight your own battle."

The soup came, and the fish. At the *entrée* Susan dropped her fork.

"Goodness gracious!" she exclaimed.

"What's the matter? Do you see Marjorie?"

"No, silly. Don't look back—please don't look back." She leaned across the table breathlessly. "Do you happen to know Dan Wilbur?"

"Don't think I ever heard of him. Is he one of your string?"

"Why, it's perfectly awful!" Susan exploded. "I refused to go to luncheon with him because I told him—I told him—gracious me!"

"What's the excitement?" insisted Lieutenant Faulkner.

Susan's lips were suddenly frozen into a smile which was not wholly forbidding, but it wasn't anything else, and she nodded over Lieutenant Faulkner's shoulder at someone behind him.

"Don't look—oh, please don't look," she pleaded desperately. "I hope—I *do* hope, he doesn't come over here."

Lieutenant Faulkner's occupation in life was obeying orders, unless perchance, he was giving them. And now he sat perfectly still, with an inquiring uplift of his brows.

"What's Mr. Wilbur going to do?" he inquired at last. "Throw a plate at us?"

"I can't tell you—I can't explain—but he's coming—he's coming—and—"

The lieutenant straightened up in his chair. He wanted to do the right thing, whatever that might be, and the deep perturbation on Susan's face indicated a need of action.

"Shall I give Mr. Wilbur a poke?" he queried.

"Oh, goodness, no!" exclaimed Susan. The lieutenant was willing, but impassive. "Just don't speak—don't say anything—don't do *any*thing! Are you sure you've never met him?"

"Well, I wouldn't take an oath that I hadn't, but—" the lieutenant began.

"Sh-h-h-h! He's coming!"

Lieutenant Faulkner proceeded calmly with the *entrée*. After a moment someone appeared beside him. He barely glanced up.

"O Dan, I'm so glad to see you again!" Susan bubbled. "I hadn't expected that—that—" and she really hadn't expected it. "Do let me introduce you. Mr. Wilbur this is—this is the lieutenant. Lieutenant, permit me—Mr. Wilbur."

Lieutenant Faulkner arose to take the proffered hand.

"I'm very glad, indeed, to meet you, Lieutenant," Mr. Wilbur assured him.

Lieutenant Faulkner considered the matter calmly, carefully, and dispassionately, as he sought some illuminating suggestion in Susan's face. But there was nothing; he was alone to struggle out the best way he could.

"Thank you," he ventured at last.

"I had the pleasure of meeting Mrs. Rowland here some years ago," Mr. Wilbur continued, "and I ran across her accidentally this morning. I presume congratulations are too late now?"

"Really, it's a matter of no consequence," replied Lieutenant Faulkner, with the utmost unconcern. "Pray, don't mention it."

Mr. Wilbur looked slightly surprised, that was all.

"I tried to induce Mrs. Rowland to permit me—" he began.

"Lieutenant, do you know what time it is?" demanded Susan suddenly. There was a warning excitement in the tone; Lieutenant Faulkner glanced up.

"No. What time is it?" he queried, as if startled.

"Our engagement you remember at half-past one, and here it is twenty minutes to two, and—"

Lieutenant Faulkner arose suddenly.

"I had no idea it was so late," he declared valiantly in deep concern. "Hadn't we better go at once?"

"Just what I was thinking," remarked Susan hurriedly. "Awfully sorry not to have seen more of you, Dan. Important engagement, you know. Awful hurry. Goodbye. Pleasant trip."

IV

(*Letter from Mrs. Paul Abercrombie Harwell Rowland, of New York, to Mrs. J. Hildegarde Stevens, of Philadelphia.*)

AT HOME, Wednesday

MY DEAR, DEAR AUNT GARDIE

"The end of the world has come. Now please, please don't scold. I didn't bring it—it just came. It descended upon me and I am absolutely overwhelmed. I feel so lost and weepy about it that I simply must ask advice. There's no one else I can ask advice of—so. It happened this way:

"You remember Dan Wilbur, don't you? You remember, too, about three years ago when he proposed to me and I refused—another one!—he went away for a tour of the world? Well, he's back. He brought the end of the world with him, and that's what's the matter. At least if he hadn't come back it wouldn't have happened.

"I was in Maillard's the other day when Dan appeared. He had just arrived the day before to sign some legal documents and close up his grandfather's estate, and told me he was going away that afternoon to San Francisco, and then to the Philippines to join the Mortons for another long cruise. We had some conversation about—about, oh, lots of things, and auntie, dear, he accused *me* of being a flirt! He didn't say it just casually, either. He insisted upon it and argued about it, and wanted to prove it, and almost did.

"Now you *know* I'm not a flirt. You know since my marriage to Paul I have tried and tried and tried to make every act of my life dignified and consistent. Whether I have or not I don't know, but I have tried, because I think every married woman should be dignified and consistent—if she can. Of course there's that horrid Mabel—but never mind!

"Anyway, Dan reminded me of that time up at Newport when he made a fool of himself (as if I could help that!) and asked all about the others. He insisted that I had flirted with him and that I had flirted with them, and that I'm a flirt now, which, of course, isn't true. He insisted so hard and said such mean things to me that I think I must have lost my temper. He was so smug and self-satisfied and complacent about it that I just hated him.

"In conclusion, he invited me to luncheon with him. It just happened that I had an engagement to luncheon with Paul, and I could not have accepted his if I had wanted to. Not that I wanted to, of course. Anyway, I could not have accepted, and I wouldn't have after all the mean things he said.

"Now he had told me positively he was going away that afternoon, so I said goodbye and we talked about not seeing each other for years and years, and then I left him to meet Paul. But instead of meeting me Paul had to go down to that horrid old Army and Navy Building to consult with somebody about something—it seems to me he spends all his life doing that—and rather than disappoint me he sent Lieutenant Faulkner to take me to Sherry's to luncheon. You know Lieutenant Faulkner, of course.

"Well, we went to Sherry's, and right in the middle of our luncheon who should appear but *Dan Wilbur*! Of all the places in the world where he might have gone, of course he had to go to Sherry's. And there was I with Lieutenant Faulkner, when I had told Dan that I was going to luncheon with my husband—he didn't know either of them, by the way—and had refused to go to luncheon with him to prove that I was not—was not that kind. I almost strangled when I saw him. You understand it wouldn't have disturbed me at all if he hadn't just accused me of all those horrid things, and here seemed to be proof of just what he had said. If he had known that Lieutenant Faulkner wasn't Paul I never could have explained it, and I should never have heard the last of it.

"So, in the middle of luncheon, here came Dan over to our table. Lieutenant Faulkner's back was toward him. When Dan came up I had to introduce them—I just *had* to—but I *didn't* introduce Lieutenant Faulkner as my husband. No, really, auntie, I didn't. I introduced him as *the lieutenant*, and, of course, if Dan wanted to jump at conclusions that was his business. I think he jumped—in fact, I know he jumped. It was dreadfully funny, really, and I would have laughed if I hadn't been so scared. But even then it didn't strike me as being so very serious, because Dan had said he was going away that afternoon to be gone for years and years, and he might never have known the difference. So, auntie, what could I have done?

"Well, anyway, I hurried out with Lieutenant Faulkner, leaving Dan to figure it out anyway he could. And now the worst is to come. I have just heard that Dan didn't go away at all; that he is to stay here a few days because of something connected with the estate, and now he'll be loose around New York with the idea in his mind that Lieutenant Faulkner is Paul, my husband, and I can't disabuse him without admitting the very things of which he has accused me. Isn't it perfectly awful? If Dan and Paul ever meet—oh, auntie!

"When I realized the matter was this serious I cried, and suggested to Paul that he was dreadfully overworked or something, and that we really ought to go away for a couple of weeks so he could rest. He laughed at me, and I can't go without him, because they might meet, anyway.

"Now, auntie, dear auntie, what shall I do? Don't take time to scold me—just tell me what I must do.

Your loving,
Sue

"P. S. Lieutenant Faulkner behaved like a brick. He's a dear!

Sue

"N. B. My new Redfern is a perfect dream, auntie dear. With the dishpan hat it's just too stunning for anything.

S.

V

(Letter from Mrs. J. Hildegarde Stevens, of Philadelphia, to Mrs. Paul Abercrombie Harwell Rowland, of New York.)

At Home, Thursday

You dear little goose

"Go instantly to your husband, to Dan Wilbur, and to Lieutenant Faulkner, and explain everything to them—everything.

Your loving,
Aunt Gardie

("Why, I couldn't do that *to save my life*!" said Susan.)

VI

C leverness in conversation doesn't necessarily consist in the number of words used. Lieutenant Faulkner, U. S. A., was demonstrating this to Miss Marjorie Stanwood. He had met her ten minutes before, and already knew the size of her glove, what flowers she preferred, and her plans for the next three months. He had discovered, too, that she was quite the most wonderful woman in the world; that unutterable things lay in the lambent eyes, and that she was born in April, the month of diamonds.

On her side, Miss Stanwood knew that Lieutenant Faulkner was an officer in the United States Army, that he came of an old F. F. V., that he had seen service in the Philippines, that he adored brown hair (her hair was brown), that he wouldn't look the second time at any woman whose eyes were not dark brown (her eyes were dark brown), and that his ideal of physical perfection in woman would weigh one hundred and twenty-seven and a half pounds, and be five feet four and a half inches tall. Strangely enough, she weighed just one hundred and twenty-seven and a half pounds, and her height was precisely five feet four and a half inches.

So it may be seen they were progressing. And without the kindly offices of Susan, too. Fortunately, or unfortunately, it had not fallen to Susan's lot to introduce them; in fact, Miss Stanwood and Susan were unknown to each other. The stately Mrs. Wetmore just happened to be acquainted with both—Lieutenant Faulkner and Miss Stanwood—and brought them together, quite unconscious of the seething turbulence which lay behind the uniform of the army man. Ever since that blissful instant when they met they had been sitting together in a nook under the stairs in earnest conversation.

"You're going to give me some dances, of course," said Lieutenant Faulkner.

"*Some* dances?" inquired Miss Stanwood.

"Yes, some, several, more than a few," explained the unabashed lieutenant. "Let me see your card."

She handed it over, and he examined it carefully.

"I'll take the second," he remarked, "and the block of four, five, six, and seven, then the ninth and the 'Home, Sweet Home.'"

"But that's all I have left," protested Miss Stanwood.

"Too bad," commented the lieutenant. "If I'd only met you a few minutes before I might have had them all. Guess that'll have to do, though."

"But, Lieutenant, really I—"

"Say, I think I know this fellow Wiggins who has the third dance," interrupted the lieutenant. "Maybe I could arrange it—"

"No," exclaimed Miss Stanwood positively. "It's perfectly ridiculous."

Suddenly she burst out laughing. Lieutenant Faulkner drew back and gazed at her in a sort of trance. It suggested rippling waters, and birds singing, and the tinkling of silver bells, and—and—it was simply immense, that's all! When the little whirlwind of merriment had passed the lieutenant drew a deep sigh.

"Remember that night at the opera?" he queried.

"What night? What opera?"

"The night I saw you first? You were sitting in a box on the second tier."

"I didn't know you had ever seen me," remarked Miss Stanwood. "When was it?"

"At the opera, that night I was there."

"But what night? What opera was it?"

Lieutenant Faulkner stared at her blankly for an instant.

"I don't remember," he confessed. "I don't think I looked at the stage after I saw you."

Miss Stanwood regarded him doubtfully for a moment while the color tingled in her cheeks.

"Surely you know the name of the opera," she insisted.

"Oh, it was that thing with the devil in it!"

Again Miss Stanwood laughed. It was the seductive harmony of a windswept lute, the gurgling coo of a dove in a shady dell, the—the— Lieutenant Faulkner nervously mopped a feverish brow.

"'Faust,'" she gasped at last. And the laugh died away. "You saw me that night? What did you think of me?"

Lieutenant Faulkner started to tell her in detail, but changed his mind. Whether it was sudden timidity or lack of a sufficient supply of roseate adjectives, doesn't appear.

"Stunning!" he declared at last, fervently. "I knew your father, of course, by sight—seen his picture, you know, and all that—but I never knew he had a daughter—at least, *such* a daughter! The moment I did know it I began to look for someone who knew the daughter, and—"

　　　　　　　　　　　　　　　　　　JACQUES FUTRELLE

He floundered helplessly and stopped. Miss Stanwood was gazing at him in frank disapproval.

"Are all army officers like you?" she demanded coldly.

"No," returned Lieutenant Faulkner readily. "Far be it for me to shower bouquets upon myself, but I may say they are not all like me."

"Really, you're a very extraordinary young man."

"Guess so," he admitted with a grin. "That's what old Sore Toe said of me once."

"Old Sore Toe?" repeated Miss Stanwood in amazement. "Pray who is he, or what is it?"

"Oh, of course, you don't know," the lieutenant apologized. "Old Sore Toe—General Underwood, that's his army name; he always has the gout."

But Lieutenant Faulkner didn't tell her why that distinguished soldier and disciplinarian had said it, which showed that the lieutenant had some semblance of modesty, for the happening which evoked the comment was one of those desperate, dare-devil undertakings of guerilla warfare when the soldier must forget, for his country's sake, the fact that life is of any particular value. These incidents are too rarely known to history. Lieutenant Faulkner was not the kind of man to write it there.

Miss Stanwood sat silent for a little while. With a vague feeling of having offended her, the lieutenant picked up the dance card mutely and stared at it.

"Say," he pleaded, "won't you please let me go shoo Wiggins off?"

"Certainly not," replied Miss Stanwood firmly, and just at that moment a partner appeared to claim her.

Lieutenant Faulkner wandered away disconsolately and chanced upon Dan Wilbur. It occurred to him that something beyond a nod was necessary, but just what it was he couldn't determine. So he nodded; that was safe, anyway.

"Where is Mrs. Rowland?" inquired Mr. Wilbur.

"Couldn't tell you," replied the lieutenant hastily. And that seemed safe.

He hurried on, glad of an opportunity to leave Mr. Wilbur alone. Mr. Wilbur stared after him a moment curiously. The lieutenant found Susan over near the door.

"Saw that Wilbur chap back there," he remarked inconsequentially.

"Here?" exclaimed Susan, and a startled expression drove the color from her face. "Oh!"

She stood with downcast eyes. The lieutenant chose to read her attitude as something more than trivial perturbation; there was apprehension in it, a haunting fear, even.

"Of course, Sue," he said uneasily, "if there's anything I can do for you so far as this chap Wilbur is concerned, all you have to do is to say so?"

"No, no," Susan explained hastily. "It's nothing that he's to blame for. It's something that I—that I—it's so hard to explain to anyone. I *can't* explain it."

"I don't want you to," replied the lieutenant sturdily. "I won't let you try. It's none of my business. It's simply if Wilbur is offensive to you I'll go tell him so."

Two limpid blue eyes were raised to the lieutenant's face gravely. There was no trace of a smile now about the taunting lips.

"Faulk, you've known me for a long time, haven't you?"

"Yes," he replied.

"Well, believe in me—don't quit believing in me. I can't explain—I won't attempt it. But really it's funny, it's awfully funny!"

And without any apparent reason, Susan burst out laughing. Lieutenant Faulkner stood staring at her blankly.

VII

M iss Stanwood and Mr. Wilbur were chatting.

"Don't you think the army dress uniform is entirely too elaborate?" she inquired casually.

Mr. Wilbur turned and glanced at Lieutenant Faulkner and Susan as they swept down the room together to the strains of a Strauss waltz.

"Well, their wives encourage it in them, I imagine," Mr. Wilbur remarked lightly. "See the worried expression on her face? She probably thinks there isn't enough gold lace."

"Oh!" exclaimed Miss Stanwood. Then, after a moment: "Is that his wife dancing with him?"

"Yes. Splendid couple, isn't it?"

When we go above a certain strata in social geology we find people who don't exhibit their emotions, but swallow them. Miss Stanwood lived in this clarified, rarefied atmosphere.

"She's beautiful!" she remarked at last.

"I dare say," Mr. Wilbur admitted listlessly.

Miss Stanwood glanced at him. Something in his tone caused her to look at him; something in his eyes caused her to look away again, and the red blood rushed to her cheeks. Five minutes later, in the same little nook under the stairs, Miss Stanwood tore her dance card into fragments. Then she went home and cried. Just like a girl!

VIII

General underwood was not the sort of a soldier who looked well at a function, but in the chaste, unostentatious uniform which he effected in action—i.e., shirt open at the throat, trousers, field glasses, and sword—he was to be reckoned among those present. He couldn't murmur a compliment into a lady's ear, but he could roar like a mad bull in the field, and every man who heard him dodged. His rank had not been handed to him upon a golden platter; he won it a trio of decades ago fighting Indians, and when need of something more than a lay figure for epaulets arose in the Philippines, General Underwood was shunted out there as a matter of course. He left an indelible imprint on the plains and sierras, and on the islands of the blue Pacific. To this day the wily red man cherishes traditions of the Great Voice; and Filipino mothers frighten their babes to sleep with stories of the mighty warrior, Much Noise.

General Underwood was Lieutenant Faulkner's master in the gentle art of war. Their first meeting, face to face and man to man, was an incident which both remembered. The general, with a fresh attack of gout, was hopping back and forth in front of service headquarters, cursing steadily, yet without haste or slovenliness, and pausing now and then to sum up results of a minor engagement through his glasses. A quarter of a mile off to his right, invisible in the tangled, tropical growth, lay a battery of light guns. The occasional flash and bang and hiss and roar of a shell was all there was to indicate the position of the battery. The objective point of fire was a Filipino stronghold which nestled in a pleasant valley below.

"Who's in command of that battery?" demanded General Underwood of an aide.

"Lieutenant Faulkner, sir."

"Bring him here."

And after a while Lieutenant Faulkner appeared. At that time he was a slender, boyish chap of twenty-two or so, and spick and span as a new silk hat. The grizzled old Indian fighter scowled at him.

"Are you a soldier?" he bellowed suddenly.

"I hope so, sir," replied Lieutenant Faulkner coldly.

"West Point?" It was a sneer.

"Yes, sir." And that was a boast.

"Well, where the hell do you think you are? At a tea party?"

Lieutenant Faulkner flushed, but didn't say.

"I suppose you think this is some pleasant little diversion arranged especially for your afternoon's amusement," General Underwood went on. "Well, it isn't, sir. We're fighting, and we're fighting for that." By a gesture he indicated the Stars and Stripes which fluttered and whipped above them. "You've a battery of four guns over there and you haven't fired a dozen shots in an hour. The order was to smash that cluster of huts. Now go back and do it, sir. Give 'em volleys, sir; pile shells on 'em; smother 'em; don't leave one stick on top of another. That's all."

"Very well, sir." And Lieutenant Faulkner returned to his post.

Three hours later he reappeared before General Underwood and stood at attention. The commanding officer glared at him; the slender, boyish figure was immaculate as ever.

"Well?" growled General Underwood.

"I should like to borrow a company of infantry, sir," replied the lieutenant.

"Company of infantry? What for?"

"To shovel off two or three layers of shells, and see if one stick is still left on top of another," replied Lieutenant Faulkner steadily. "And, meanwhile, here's an army manual which gives the proper form of address between *gentlemen*. You might find it useful."

General Underwood glared straight into the imperturbable eyes of the youngster for a moment, with slowly rising color. He started to say something violent, but changed his mind.

"It teaches the common or garden variety of etiquette," supplemented the lieutenant coldly.

General Underwood turned and entered his tent. A few minutes later he reappeared; Lieutenant Faulkner still stood as he had left him. The elder man went over and laid one hand on his shoulder.

"You and I were educated in different schools," he said slowly. "Mine taught action, yours action according to a standard. Both are good. But if you intend to stick to the army, my boy, you must learn the value of quantity. Shoot straight, but shoot often, too. If one shot is good, two shots are better, three are better still. It's a rule which applies to all things. Remember it."

And so—

At ten o'clock on the morning following the Sanger ball, Lieutenant Faulkner sent a box of violets to Miss Marjorie Stanwood;

at noon he sent a box of roses; at two o'clock he sent a box of carnations; and at four he called in person. It was a fusillade. An austere servant took his card and disappeared.

"Miss Stanwood is not in," the servant returned to say.

The clear eyes of the army man studied the stolid, melancholy face intently for an instant.

"Not in, or—not in?" he inquired. There was a difference as he said it.

"Miss Stanwood is not in," repeated the servant. There was no difference as he said it.

Lieutenant Faulkner went down the steps with thoughtfully squinting eyes, and the door closed behind him. He paused irresolutely at the corner and glanced back at the white marble facade of the palace he had just left. *Phew!* What a home! It awed him a little as he looked. Eighteen hundred a year, and *she* lived in *that*! For the first time in his life, perhaps, Lieutenant Faulkner was aroused to a full appreciation of his own splendid nerve.

He was just starting to go about his business when he saw a young man start up the front steps of the palace. Dan Wilbur! Of course!

"Now something tells me that he isn't going in there to call on father," soliloquized the lieutenant grimly. "We'll just see what happens."

Mr. Wilbur disappeared inside. Of course Lieutenant Faulkner wouldn't have allowed anything like vulgar curiosity to anchor him on that corner for five minutes, but you understand there was a chance that Mr. Wilbur would be right out again, and in that event they might stroll down the street together. No; on second thoughts he couldn't have anything to say to Mr. Wilbur, because—because—well, anyway he waited.

Ten minutes or so passed, then a pair of heavily embroidered wrought iron gates adjoining the palace swung inward, and a huge touring car emerged. It edged along the curb and stopped at the steps. Lieutenant Faulkner watched it with singular misgivings. The palace door yawned, and gave up—Marjorie Stanwood. Of course! He knew it! He stood staring, staring dumbly, while a queer sense of hunger crept over him. It was the sort of feeling he used to have when he stood around on one foot watching mother make pies.

Marjorie didn't walk down the steps, she floated down, a radiant shimmery creature in some champagney looking stuff. She paused on the bottom step and smiled up into the face of—yes, it was Dan Wilbur. He said something and she laughed outright with a charming back-tilt of her head. Then Mr. Wilbur handed her into the automobile, stepped in beside her, and closed the door behind him. The car whirred and swung wide to turn.

Suddenly Lieutenant Faulkner awoke to a realization of the fact that he was—well, a small boy would have called it "rubbering." The car was turning toward the spot where he stood. He took three backward steps, and there, screened by the jutting building, straightened his tie, braced himself, and turned the corner with the utmost carelessness just as the car glided by slowly.

He met Miss Stanwood's eyes fairly, smiled, and lifted his cap. She did not even take the trouble to avert her gaze, merely regarded him for a moment with a steady stare that sent the blood to his face, then turned and looked the other way. The car passed on.

IX

Lieutenant Faulkner called on Susan. He found her with reddened, tear-stained eyes, and altogether in a charming state of unhappiness. She welcomed him with something like tragic enthusiasm, then went over and hid her face in a pillow and wept shamelessly. He sat down glumly, despondently, and looked at her. Nothing was of any consequence anymore.

"What's the matter, Sue?" he asked dutifully after a time.

"O Faulk!" she wailed, "you can't imagine—you simply can't imagine—what has happened to me."

"Well, whatever it is it isn't a marker to what has happened to *me*," he returned solemnly.

The frightful disaster which had overtaken Susan was easily explained. She had been constrained to decline a dinner invitation because Dan Wilbur was to be one of the guests. Now she scented some new horror in Lieutenant Faulkner's statement, and sat up straight in sudden alarm.

"You have seen Dan Wilbur!" she declared tragically.

"I have," returned the lieutenant hopelessly.

"Oh-h-h!" exclaimed Susan, only it was longer than that. "I knew it would come. I knew it!"

The lieutenant regarded her with a mild surprise which almost amounted to interest.

"Knew what would come?" he inquired.

"Didn't he tell you?" she demanded breathlessly.

"I didn't talk with him," explained the lieutenant. "I merely saw him. That was enough for me."

Susan regarded him dully for a moment, then laughed a hysterical, high-pitched laugh that startled the lieutenant a little.

"What are you talking about, Faulk?" she asked, after a moment.

Lieutenant Faulkner leaned back in his chair, clasped both hands about one knee, and stared at Susan thoughtfully.

"Sue," he asked slowly, after a pause, "you've always found me a fair specimen of a self-respecting white man, haven't you?"

"Of course, yes."

"An individual who possesses a certain outward semblance of a decent gentleman?"

"Yes."

"You never saw me eat soup with a fork?"

Susan nearly smiled.

"No," she replied.

"Or wear tan shoes with evening dress?"

"No, of course not." "What—?"

"Or a silk hat with a sack coat?"

"Certainly not," Susan answered impatiently. "What *are* you talking about?"

"On the whole, what do you think of me?"

The lieutenant was rocking back and forth slowly with his eyes fixed on Susan's face. He was perfectly serious about it; he wanted to know.

"I think," replied Susan, and she remembered a little scene in Sherry's a day or so before, "I think you are just splendid!"

Lieutenant Faulkner was too much preoccupied to blush.

"You don't feel it necessary to lock up the silver when I call, do you?" he pursued.

Susan laughed outright.

"Well, why should a person to whom I have been formally introduced—whom I have met on her own level—cut me dead, as if I were a doormat thief?" inquired the lieutenant.

"Cut you?" repeated Susan, aghast.

"I looked straight into the eyes of the only woman I ever loved—at least, *one* of the only women I ever loved—and it was like a trip to the North Pole," he explained. "She simply looked at me, and I wasn't there. It was precisely as if she were gazing out of an open window."

"You mean Miss Stanwood?" Susan inquired, as a matter of fact.

"I mean Marjorie," replied the lieutenant. It was such a delicious, mouth filling name. "I told you last night about meeting her, and taking all her left-over dances, and how she went home suddenly, and I didn't get any of them. Well, I called this afternoon. She wasn't 'in.' I took that as a formal way of telling me she was not receiving, and rather imagined she was ill—from her sudden disappearance last night. Ten minutes later she came out and got into an automobile. I saluted her—it was like making overtures to an ice-cream freezer." There was a pause. "Dan Wilbur was with her."

"Dan Wilbur!" Susan's own private, individual troubles came rushing back upon her, and she put her head in the pillow again. After a little while she straightened up with the air of a martyr. "Are you sure she saw you?"

"Saw me?" exclaimed the lieutenant. "When you hold both handles of a battery you know when the electricity is on, don't you? Well, the electricity was on. Now, why?"

"She might not have recognized you," Susan ventured.

"I don't want to boast, Sue, but she'll never forget me."

There was a long, long pause.

"There is always one answer, of course," Susan said at last sympathetically. "That is, that she doesn't care to continue the acquaintance."

"Acquaintance!" repeated the lieutenant. "Why, Sue, we're friends—old friends. Why I've known Marjorie Stanwood since—since 'way last night about nine o'clock." He passed one hand across a troubled brow. "Sue, you were not present at the preliminaries," he added reproachfully. "It was the prettiest get away you ever saw."

Again there was silence. Susan arose and rearranged some flowers in a spindle-legged vase, then sat down again. Lieutenant Faulkner continued to stare at her musingly.

"It's the money, I suppose," he said slowly after a time. "Funny what it does, isn't it? Great-grandfather is hanged for stealing sheep; grandfather discovers how to make a fairly good sort of axle grease out of the sheep scraps, and gets rich doing it; which makes father the millionaire axle-grease and butter king. Then son comes along and converts the whole shooting match, from claws to feathers, into imported olive oil, and rigs up a family tree to suit himself. Grandson is so superior he won't look at anybody on the same planet. Money does it. Isn't it—isn't it filthy?"

Susan was regarding him with a little perplexed pucker on her white brow. With variations she knew a dozen families to whom the simile generally applied, although it would never have occurred to her in just that light.

"I suppose if Stanwood knew I was in love with his daughter," the lieutenant continued, "and that my income was eighteen hundred a year—not a minute, like his—he'd froth at the mouth and get out an injunction."

Susan thoughtfully plucked a flower and thrust it into her shimmering hair. The bottomless eyes were fixed unseeingly on one of the lieutenant's epaulets.

"And yet Marjorie—Marjorie," he rolled the word under his tongue, "Marjorie isn't that kind of a girl. She was as simple and unaffected and ingenuous as—why, Sue, you ought to have met her. And when she laughed!" The lieutenant arose suddenly and strode back and forth across the room. "Why, hang it, she *isn't* that kind of a girl," he declared stoutly. "You can't imagine her sticking her nose into the air just because father has money. And far be it from me to say anything *about* father, but if he got it like the muckrakers say he did, he ought to go dig a hole and bury it."

"Well, of course *my* father—" Susan began defensively.

"Oh, your father," the lieutenant cut in ungraciously. "His money is in and came out of real estate. I'm talking about those chaps who made their money last Thursday or Friday by grinding down the affluent widows and taking it away from indiscreet orphans." He was silent a moment. "I know that Marjorie isn't that kind, and if she isn't—what's the answer?"

He sat down and stared gloomily out of the window.

"I'm sorry for you, Faulk," Susan sympathized finally. "I know—"

"Sorry for me? What for?"

"Of course," Susan hurried on tactfully, "Miss Stanwood is heiress to millions, and she meets a great many men with whom it is not desirable to—to—oh, you know what I mean, Faulk? Practically any man she comes across would marry her for her money if nothing else, and so—" She broke off and waved her hands comprehensively.

The lieutenant stared at her coldly, and the pupils of his eyes contracted to pin points.

"Money has never meant anything to me, Sue," he said deliberately. "I wouldn't be in the army if it did. There's nothing in it financially, even at the top, and I could cut loose and go into business. But this is a man's life, a clean, active, wholesome existence with the sort of work I like, and an opportunity to do things. I'm going to stick to it." He rolled a cigarette; Susan nodded and he lighted it. "Of course I don't know what Marjorie will have to say about it," he went on slowly, "but she is going to be Mrs. Lieutenant Faulkner. *Sabe?*"

Susan smiled a little and shrugged her shoulders.

"I imagine that Papa Stanwood will be overjoyed when he hears it," the lieutenant went on. "It may even be a cue for him to put the screws on the widows and orphans again. As a matter of fact, he can take his money and go start a fire with it if he likes; Marjorie is the girl for me. I'll take her in spite of her money."

"You speak as if you knew that she loved you," remarked Susan.

"Love me?" repeated the lieutenant. "She can't help it. I'm just crazy about her."

Susan waved her hands; the matter was beyond her.

"And this right on top of the cut direct," she commented. "Why, she has shut the gate on you in the very beginning."

"There's something behind that cut direct," mused Lieutenant Faulkner. "I don't know what it is, but it doesn't matter. And so far as shutting the gate—I'll climb over that, and tunnel under the dungeon, and shin up the lightning rod, and break down the barriers, and scale the walls, and swim the moat, and all the other usual things. Sue, she's mine, I tell you. It's my first choose, and I choose Marjorie. I guess you never saw me in action?"

Susan didn't say anything else. There didn't seem to be anything left to say. She herself had had some experience with a bull-headed army man, and the result was that now she was Mrs. Paul Abercrombie Harwell Rowland, and perfectly delighted everytime she remembered it.

"Now, of course, you'll have to help," continued Lieutenant Faulkner, as a matter of course. He arose and paced back and forth across the room to plan the campaign.

"Help?" gasped Susan. "How?"

"Well, for instance, the first thing to do," he told her in his most businesslike manner, "is to get to Marjorie. You'll have to call on her."

"But I don't know her," Susan protested. "I've never met her. I never even saw her but once."

"Pooh! Pooh!" Lieutenant Faulkner blew away this objection with one breath. "There are a thousand ways for you to get to her, that I couldn't use. Just call—er—you know how—er—er—just call." He paused helplessly. "I'll tell you," he went on suddenly, "get her interested in a charity or something, and—and you know, I—I—well, just sort of mention me, and later on I'll just casually appear, and—and, you know."

"Why, Faulk!" Susan reproved. "It's entirely out of the question. I—I—why, I can't."

"Ah, help a chap just this once, won't you?" he pleaded. "That's the way with people when they get married. They never want to give another fellow a helping hand; just sit back and grin at him and let him fight it out the best way he can. Just this once!"

Susan drew a long sigh of resignation; Faulk was such a charming boy after all.

"I'll do what I can," she said. It was a promise.

"That's the girl," and the lieutenant shook her hand heartily. "And now, of course, we've got to find out just where Wilbur is in this game. If he is interested in Marjorie he loses."

"Dan Wilbur!" Susan repeated, and suddenly there was a little catch in her voice. Temporarily she had lost sight of her own affairs. Her eyes dropped from Faulkner's eager face, and she was silent.

"Sue, what is this Wilbur thing, anyhow?" Faulkner asked gently. He took hold of her hand again.

"Nothing, Faulk, nothing," and still she looked down.

There was a long, embarrassing pause.

"Look at me, Sue," he commanded.

She raised her eyes shyly—moist, limpid eyes—and met the grave stare of the army man for one long minute without flinching. He drew a long breath and brushed back from her brow a vagrant wisp of gold.

"If there's anything the matter?" he suggested questioningly. "If I can help anyway? If you've made any mistake?"

She shook her head.

"Hadn't you better tell me?" he persisted.

"Tell you!" and Susan's red lips trembled into a smile. "Why, Faulk, you're the one man in the world that I *couldn't* tell! And it's nothing, really—a little matter of principle with me. Don't think anything else."

"Does Paul know?" he queried.

"And he's the *other* man in the world that I couldn't tell," Susan complained.

Her eyes filled and slowly her head sank forward. Faulkner felt her fingers close suddenly on his own, and then a teardrop wet his hand.

X

A nd Dan Wilbur called on Susan, too. At sight of him she shuddered twice—once for the catastrophe which would have been precipitated had he walked in ten minutes previously and found Lieutenant Faulkner; and once for the unspeakable disaster now impending, for Paul was due home in half an hour from that everlasting Army and Navy Building, and—and—

"For goodness sake, Dan Wilbur, aren't you ever going away?" she demanded by way of greeting.

"Why?" he inquired languidly. "Does my staying in New York annoy you?"

"Oh, not that, of course," Susan hastened to say. "But—but I understood you were going, and it surprises me to see you hanging about this dull, wretched old town when—oh, you know!" she concluded helplessly. She glanced at the clock—5.35.

"Surely you don't find it dull? A woman like you?"

"Why, Dan, I'm positively unhappy," she replied, truthfully enough. "There's nowhere to go, no one to see, nothing to amuse one, nothing to interest oneself in—just this same old eternal sixes and sevens."

"Well, if everything is as dull as all that I have some good news for you," said Mr. Wilbur graciously.

Susan gulped hard.

"What is it?" she demanded suspiciously.

"Well, for one thing, I've decided to stay here, and—"

Susan nearly fainted.

"Stay in New York!" she gasped tragically.

"Yes, and I'll undertake to furnish something to interest you, too—as pretty a little romance as you—"

"O Dan, Dan!" Susan interrupted wailingly. "Give up that beautiful trip around the world for—for—just to stay here in prosaic old New York?" she added diplomatically.

"It is a splendid trip," he agreed, "jolly, too, but you see—"

"Beautiful!" Susan rushed on enthusiastically. "Think of it! The Philippines! and Japan! and China! It must be glorious out there where the—er—er—and all those other places." Why couldn't she remember them?

"But you see," Mr. Wilbur explained, "I've just been on the trip once.

And, now, Sue," his voice dropped confidentially, "New York has a new attraction for me, and if things go as I wish I shall remain here, for several months at least."

Susan collapsed hopelessly into a chair and glanced at the clock.

"Another love affair, of course," she remarked.

"Another!" and Mr. Wilbur smiled that same superior sort of a smile that had hounded her into this mess in the first place. "No, not another. It's the first—the first time I've ever really loved a woman, and—"

"Why, Dan Wilbur, I'll ask you to remember, please, that you proposed to me four times," she interrupted indignantly. "And if I'm not mistaken you used that same phrase. You might at least have changed the words around some."

It was Mr. Wilbur's turn to blush; he did it languidly.

"The proposals to me were merely for amusement, I suppose?" Susan went on mercilessly. "Or was it practice?"

"But, Great Scott, Sue," Mr. Wilbur burst out eloquently, "this is *serious*!"

"And the others weren't," Susan added. "I suspected as much. Who is it, please?"

"Well, I've known her for several years," Mr. Wilbur explained with exasperating deliberation. "She was a slender little debutante three years ago, but now—"

"Skinny, you mean. All debutantes are. Go on."

"But, now, she's the most stunning—er—er—I saw her at the Sanger ball last night, and she simply knocked my eye out, that's all. Beautiful, charming, and all that, you know."

"Of course," Susan agreed impatiently, and she glanced ostentatiously at the clock. "Goodness, isn't it late? Who is she?"

"Miss Stanwood—Marjorie Stanwood. Do you know her?"

"Marj—Miss Stan—!" and Susan's surprise ended in speechlessness.

Mr. Wilbur regarded her anxiously.

"Am I to take this merely as astonishment, or—or pleasure—or—what?" he inquired.

"Marjorie Stanwood!" Susan repeated, and then she laughed nervously. The hands of the clock were fairly spinning around—5.41. "Dan, really, you must drop in again sometime and tell me all about it," she urged.

"That's just what I came in to do now," said Mr. Wilbur, without moving. "I've simply got to talk about it, that's all. I can't hold it anymore, and—and I haven't told her yet, of course, so—Say, you and your husband must come along out to dinner with me, and we'll talk it over."

"No!" It was the nearest thing to a shriek that Susan was ever guilty of; she was on her feet instantly. "No, no, Dan. Really, we couldn't accept your invitation; no, not today, or—" and she stopped.

"Why not?" demanded Mr. Wilbur stolidly. "I'd rather like a chance to get better acquainted with your husband. You know I've never had an opportunity of saying more than a word to him. It occurred to me that later on you two and Miss Stanwood might all have dinner with me some evening. She's charming."

"It's sweet of you, Dan, awfully sweet of you," said Susan, and she chose that Mr. Wilbur should read some vague, secret sorrow in her tone; "but you—you don't know Paul," which was true, "and—and— why, Dan, if he should come into this room now and find you here you simply can't imagine what a painful scene it would be for me," which was also true. "You don't understand, Dan," and *that* was true, too.

The listlessness passed out of Mr. Wilbur's eyes; he was genuinely surprised.

"Why, Sue, my dear girl!" he exclaimed, and there was an indignant note of sympathy in his voice. "Whom did you marry? An ogre?"

Susan smiled sadly and shot a furtive glance at the clock—5.44.

"Don't ask me, Dan, don't ask me! You know how gay and happy I've been all my life." He did. "I try to be the same now. It seems to have been my lot to marry Paul, and I am content." And *that* was true. "But see how late it is, Dan."

There was an irresistible note of pleading in her voice, a wistfulness in the bottomless blue eyes, entreaty in her every movement. Mr. Wilbur arose, a little dazed.

"So he is that sort of a chap, is he?" he inquired, and it was not a compliment. "I wondered. He seemed rather odd. You know the day I met him at Sherry's he impressed me strangely, and I've seen him once or twice since." He was silent a moment; the clock said 5.47. "Sue, how do you tolerate such a man?" he demanded.

"Sh-h-h-h!" and Susan raised one charming finger to her red, red lips. "He will be here in five minutes or so. It will be far best if he doesn't see you here; perhaps best that you don't call again. You understand. I can't help it, Dan," she added desperately. "Forgive me!"

"I'm sorry, Sue," said Mr. Wilbur earnestly. "I'm sorry."

Mr. Wilbur gathered up the fragments of a shattered delusion and bore them down the stairs. And this was the burden Sue's devotion had won! This was the thing she was struggling under! And all this was hidden beneath the charming, careless exterior! Poor little girl! A man had to take his life in his hands when he got married! And a woman, too! Which reminded him of Miss Stanwood!

As Mr. Wilbur passed down the front steps of the huge apartment house into the street he met another man coming in, a black-mustached, businesslike individual, a lieutenant in the United States Army by his uniform. He was square and soldierly from the tips of his boots to the top of his black head, with a keen, determined face, and shrewd penetrating eyes, which were softened tremendously by quizzical lines about the mouth. Mr. Wilbur noticed the army man merely because he had been discussing an army man, and the uniform attracted his attention.

Still musing, he walked across to the Waldorf garage to get a car for a short spin through the park before he sat down to a lonely dinner. It just happened that when he entered the office of the garage the single attendant there was in conversation with another man—a lieutenant in the United States Army by his uniform.

"I want a car that'll move," the uniformed man was saying, "something that'll leave a scorched odor behind it, and a chauffeur who won't mind the smell."

The attendant smiled politely.

"How long will you want it, sir?"

"Three or four hours—maybe all night—I don't know," was the reply. "I'm going up Tarrytown way to dinner, and I'm liable to tear the top soil off the whole state before I get back."

"Well, we have a six-cylinder run-about in now," said the attendant. "There's just enough room for you and the chauffeur."

"That'll do," commented the army man.

"And if there's any fine, of course—?" suggested the attendant.

"It's on me. I understand."

The attendant spoke over the uniformed man's shoulder to Mr. Wilbur.

"In just a moment, sir."

The uniformed man glanced back. It was Lieutenant Faulkner.

"Good-evening," said Mr. Wilbur.

"Hello!" returned the lieutenant, and he followed the attendant out.

Mr. Wilbur went away and sat down in a café and held his head.

XI

(*Letter from Mrs. Paul Abercrombie Harwell Rowland, of New York, to Mrs. J. Hildegarde Stevens, of Philadelphia.*)

AT HOME, Friday

MY DEAR, DEAR AUNT GARDIE

"I just can't, that's all. I've tried and tried and *tried*. It just won't come. Everytime I look at Lieutenant Faulkner or Dan Wilbur or Paul, I'm sure I'm going to die of mortification. I'm in such a nervous, scary condition that if either of them said 'Boo' to me, I *know* I'd die. And as for telling either of them! Auntie, dear auntie, I can't. And things are getting worse every moment, because Dan Wilbur isn't ever going around the world anymore—he's staying here.

"Lieutenant Faulkner was here this afternoon. He knows I'm terribly worried about something, and like the dear, good fellow he is, he wants to help; but he doesn't dream what it is. If he should suddenly find out! He gave me every opportunity to tell him, and believe me, auntie, I tried. I had it on the tip of my tongue a dozen times, and everytime it stuck right there. It wouldn't come out. Just think of saying to him casually: 'I made Dan Wilbur believe you were my husband. Ha, ha, ha!' Isn't it awful? And if I should try to lead up to it, it would make it seem more important than I should want him to think I think it, so there. Auntie, dear, imagine yourself picking out the very nicest young man of your acquaintance, and saying such a thing to him! Or explaining it to Uncle Steve!

"And Dan Wilbur was here, too. He just missed Lieutenant Faulkner as he came in, and just missed Paul as he went out. Br-r-r-r! I simply had to shoo him off to keep him from meeting Paul. He was for taking us out to dinner! Think of it! And I tried to tell him, too. Yes I did, auntie dear, and I couldn't. Instead of that I went on and on trying to get him away, and I know he must think frightful things of Paul. But, really, it isn't my fault, and I didn't tell him an untruth, even a little one. I dare say Dan won't ever come to see us anymore.

JACQUES FUTRELLE

"I was hysterical when Paul came in. Why he must have passed Dan in the hall. Think of *that*! I just ran and threw my arms around his neck and cried on him terribly, Paul, I mean. Naturally he wanted to know what was the matter, and that frightened me more than ever. I drew away from him and looked at him, and my conscience gave me such a fearful jab that I resolved to tell him then and there.

"'Paul, you must know—' I started. And then I stammered and cried all over again, and he kissed me. Then, somehow, he got it into his head that I was crying because I was dissatisfied with a new gown that came today, and—well, I'm just letting him think so yet. I know I never will be brave enough to start it all over again.

"But here's a scheme; it just occurred to me. Now listen carefully:

"Lieutenant Faulkner is dreadfully in love with Marjorie Stanwood. Yes, the heiress—it's the same one. Of course Faulk hasn't a penny, but—Paul didn't have a great deal. Faulk and I talked it over this afternoon, and he's determined to have her, and he ought to have her if he wants her. He's frightfully smitten, violent about it, you understand. Dan Wilbur is in love with her, too, in a fishy sort of a way. Think of it! Those two men above all others on earth. That's why Dan gave up his trip around the world; he's going to stay here and try to win Miss Stanwood.

"Well! I believe, as they say in politics, I can exercise a great deal of influence in the affair in ways which would be too tedious to explain. I'm going to try to do it—help Lieutenant Faulkner. You see, if I help Faulk, and he wins, Miss Stanwood will send Dan Wilbur about his business, and the sooner Faulk wins the sooner she will send Dan Wilbur about his business. Do you see the point? Then Dan would go on around the world, as he planned, and everything would be all right. By the time he got back everything would be so far away it would be a joke, anyway.

"Now, isn't that a good scheme, if I can do it? And do you see how simple it would make it for me? I wouldn't have to explain to anybody, and I could look all my friends in the face again without feeling that I must cry. I'm going to call on

Miss Stanwood tomorrow, and start the ball rolling. What do you think of it, auntie, dear?

"Do write soon.

Your loving,
SUE

"P. S.—It's nearly midnight, and I'm writing this in my own room. Paul is in the next room, sound asleep and *snoring*! Isn't it unromantic to snore? Now I must run out and drop this in the mail chute. Goodnight.

SUE

"N. B.—Marjorie Stanwood is really and truly stunning, but it wouldn't do any good to let the men know I think it.

S.

(And from that moment Dan Wilbur never had a chance, so far as Susan was concerned.)

XII

The footman stood waiting. Miss Marjorie Stanwood turned the card over thoughtfully and stared at the back. Then she read it again: "Mrs. Paul Abercrombie Harwell Rowland." The name seemed vaguely familiar; it was elusive. She couldn't place it. Perhaps the Blue Book! Yes. "Mrs. Paul Abercrombie Harwell Rowland (née Courtenay, Susan Isabel)." Sue Courtenay, of course!

"Tell Mrs. Rowland I'll be down in a moment," she instructed.

And five minutes later she followed her message to the drawing-room. At the door she paused and stared—yes, positively stared. And then her eyes dropped to the card which she carried in her hand. Yes, the name was Rowland—Mrs. Paul Abercrombie Harwell Rowland. Miss Stanwood came forward uncertainly with an unconscious uplift of her charming chin.

"I think you must have—I think there must be some mistake in the card?" she remarked. "Doubtless you sent me the wrong one. I understood it was Mrs. Rowland?"

"I am Mrs. Rowland," Susan explained, with an inquiring slant of her brows.

Miss Stanwood stopped still and stared at her again. There was no mistaking it—it was a stare. First there was uneasiness in it, then something closely akin to bewilderment, after which came a wonderfully illuminating smile, and Miss Stanwood impulsively extended both hands to her caller.

"How stupid of me!" she exclaimed. "You were Miss Courtenay, weren't you—*the* Sue Courtenay?"

And Susan was her friend for life.

"I had always wanted so much to see you," Miss Stanwood went on naïvely. "I did see you the other evening at the Sanger ball, but somehow you were not associated in my mind with *the* Miss Courtenay. And the name, Mrs. Rowland, was quite—quite strange to me. I didn't understand that you were Mrs.—Mrs. Rowland!"

For the first time in her life, perhaps, Susan felt that she didn't know the right thing to say. She didn't blame Lieutenant Faulkner a bit for falling in love with this girl; nor Dan Wilbur, either, for that matter. Whatever she said was commonplace, so it doesn't matter.

"Even in the finishing school days we used to be interested in you and what you did," Miss Stanwood continued smilingly. Her hand still lay in Susan's. "You can't imagine what a fruitful source of discussion you were, and I'm afraid there was envy in it, too. Do you mind?"

And after that how could Susan bring the conversation around to so commonplace a thing as Lieutenant Faulkner? The formal call degenerated into a sociable little visit—girl to girl. Susan did make a pretense, twice, of talking of some charity which had never entered her mind until that moment, but Miss Stanwood agreed to help so readily that it didn't even furnish a subject for conversation.

Half an hour later Susan went her way. And then she began to grow ashamed of herself, for *Lieutenant Faulkner's name had not been mentioned!* It was not so bad, of course, because this new and sudden friendship opened up future possibilities of discussion, and then—

Lieutenant Faulkner called at five o'clock. Susan put on a deeply penitent expression and went into the drawing room to meet him. He was pacing back and forth with his hands in his pockets, and a triumphant smile on his face.

"Faulk, I'm awfully sorry—" she began demurely.

He turned.

"Sue, you're the best ever," he declared. "They can't beat you." He shook both her hands; she was positive he was going to kiss her. "When I go out I'll send you a truckful of—of—say, what sort of flowers do you like, anyway?"

Susan merely waited.

"See?" the lieutenant rattled on. "It was at my place when I came from the office?"

He produced a small envelope and drew a card from it; Susan read it:

"Miss Stanwood regrets that she was not at home when Lieutenant Faulkner called. She will be pleased to receive Lieutenant Faulkner on Monday, at four."

And positively Susan hadn't mentioned his name to her!

XIII

There are two ways to win the heart of a woman—the way everybody else does it, and someother way. The principal difference between Dan Wilbur and Lieutenant Faulkner was that Dan Wilbur chose the first way. It was only natural that he should, since the whole of his idle life had been devoted to learning the rules. One could never have the slightest doubt of what he would do in an emergency—it would be the proper thing, done gracefully, win or lose. He was the well-bred gentleman, trimmed to pattern with the raw edges turned under and sewed. And thus he was a counterpart of every other man in the "Social Register," this being a compliment to the "Social Register."

Lieutenant Faulkner played the game according to the rules, trump for trump, so long as the rules seemed to adequately cover the particular condition to which they were applied. But he was liable to introduce a dazzling variation at any moment; finesse a five-spot, for instance, while the other players looked on with their mouths open. There was a certain exhilaration in following his game, because it was so different. His code of play was beyond criticism; it was merely that he played faster. And he'd never had an idle moment in his life; there was too much fun living.

Now the little daughters of the rich are cast about by many strange conventions. Dan Wilbur knew them, accepted them as a matter of course, and was bound by them. They never occurred to Lieutenant Faulkner, and probably wouldn't have disturbed him much if they had. So, starting at the same time with the same goal in view, they went by widely deviating paths. At the end of four days they were out of sight of each other, and going in opposite directions.

For instance, Mr. Wilbur spent a quiet, thoughtful Sunday, considering the subject of marriage as related to himself. Matrimony is a condition which has its advantages and its disadvantages. Mr. Wilbur reviewed them all, carefully weighing every jot of evidence, pro and con, as it presented itself. In the summing up the weight of evidence seemed to be on the side of matrimony, and an impartial mind rendered a tentative verdict of marriage. Lieutenant Faulkner spent the same Sunday inditing sonnets to a lady's eyebrows.

On Monday Mr. Wilbur took his second forward step—went down town to consult his attorney, one Simon Degross, a shiny, semirespectable appearing little man of indeterminate age, who made a specialty of handling the business affairs of rich young men who were too idle to handle them for themselves.

"Just what is my income, Mr. Degross?" Mr. Wilbur inquired as a starter.

"Last year it was twenty-eight thousand, seven hundred and ten dollars and forty-three cents," replied the little man, much as if he had been sitting there waiting, after due preparation, to answer that particular question.

"That all?" commented Mr. Wilbur with a slight frown. "Not a great deal, is it? How much will be added to that by my share of my grandfather's estate when it is settled up?"

"Not more than seven thousand a year."

"That'll be about thirty-five thousand, won't it?" Mr. Wilbur went over and looked out of the window. "I've about decided to get married, Mr. Degross," he volunteered after a moment, "and that seems a pitifully small sum to insure a woman's life happiness, doesn't it?"

The little man shrugged his slim shoulders.

"It's altogether as you look at it," he answered. "It's a great deal to a woman who has been accustomed to less, and a pittance to one who has been accustomed to more."

"That's just the trouble," Mr. Wilbur went on. "She has been accustomed to more—a great deal more. There's no way of increasing it, I suppose?"

"Not with perfect safety," replied the lawyer. "As it is now, your money is well invested, all in first mortgages and bonds, but of course—?"

"No," interrupted Mr. Wilbur decisively. He was thoughtfully silent for a long time. "You see, I use about twenty-five thousand a year myself," he complained, "and half of the luxuries of the world are beyond me. For instance, a yacht is out of the question; and everytime I buy a new automobile I have to go easy on my other expenses. And a chap must have a new car every year or so. It's a confounded nuisance, isn't it?"

Mr. Degross didn't venture to say.

"And a wife!" Mr. Wilbur went on musingly. "What do you think?"

"I'm only a lawyer," Mr. Degross remarked modestly.

Mr. Wilbur's listless eyes were shadowed by uncertainty.

"Of course a few thousands will fix up the old place on Eighty-first Street, and I suppose we could lease some sort of a cottage at Newport for a time, still—" And again he was silent. "Why, hang it, I feel like a pauper," he declared at last. "But I'll risk it—I'll risk it. You see it isn't as if I were marrying a girl who had nothing of her own. Yes, I'll risk it."

Mr. Degross smiled faintly. When he left home that morning Mrs. Degross was changing a bird on last winter's hat to the other side.

"It's disagreeable to feel—feel positively poor, isn't it?" Mr. Wilbur inquired with a slight smile. "And she is not used to poverty in any form. It's Miss Stanwood, you know—Marjorie Stanwood."

"Indeed?" and Mr. Degross lifted his brows politely.

"I dare say there'll be a fat dowry; still, that shouldn't count," Mr. Wilbur went on in self-extenuation. "A chap ought to stand on his own feet, don't you think? I suppose we could scrape along somehow on thirty-five thousand?"

"I dare say," Mr. Degross ventured.

Lieutenant Faulkner didn't have to waste anytime computing *his* income. He *knew* it was eighteen hundred a year. So while Mr. Wilbur was in conference with his attorney, the lieutenant called on Marjorie Stanwood and held her hand so long she had to take it away from him. He made her tell him that she had not recognized him from the automobile, and didn't notice that she said it with deep reluctance. When he left her an hour later he would have reported progress.

On Tuesday Mr. Wilbur took a third step forward—went up and looked over the old house in Eighty-first Street. It needed repairs, but altogether it was better than he thought. A few odd thousands in woodwork and paint and decorations would do wonders for it. Then and there he devised new color schemes for the dining and drawing-rooms, and of course Miss Stanwood would have some suggestions. The work could be completed in six months; it wouldn't be half bad. Mr. Wilbur was growing optimistic.

He had luncheon at his club, and lingered an hour or more over his coffee. And then he had an inspiration. Harry Belknap wasn't using his cottage on the Cliff Drive; perhaps he could be induced to lease it for a time. It would be ideal there, overlooking Narragansett Bay, and rather inexpensive, too. Twelve—at the most fourteen—thousand ought to tide him over the brief Newport season with a little economy. By George, he'd write to Belknap and ask him about the place. It was small, of course, only sixteen rooms, still they could make it do; love in a cottage. And the stables would make an ideal garage. He'd have to begin economizing, though, right now. On second thought he wouldn't take another pot of coffee.

En route down town Mr. Wilbur dropped in at the florist's where some orchids had attracted his attention, stopped at the Empire and reserved a box for John Drew on Thursday, and telephoned to Sherry's to reserve his favorite table after the theater that evening. He would arrange a formal dinner party later on in Miss Stanwood's honor. And speaking of a dinner party reminded him of Susan. And Susan reminded him of a whole procession of things! For instance, he caught himself wondering as to the identity of the dark-mustached army officer whom he had met as he came out of the apartment house where Susan lived. There was no reason why he should have wondered, but he did. There were several odd things in this connection, and he reviewed them all.

Lieutenant Faulkner spent that same Tuesday in trying to figure out whether Marjorie would consider it impetuous of him if he came right out and told her he was crazy about her; also he read "Romeo and Juliet" for the first time since his school days, when he had been madly infatuated with his teacher, a widow aged thirty-one. In addition to which he made a mental note to take Marjorie to see John Drew. All men, when they are in love, take their heart's desire to see John Drew.

On Wednesday afternoon Mr. Wilbur took the plunge. He dropped in at Mr. Stanwood's office down town, and in a few chaste, unemotional words, asked permission to pay his attentions to Miss Stanwood. He was quite calm and plain-spoken and frank about it. He pointed out that he loved her more than all the world, *et cetera, et cetera*; that his regard for her had come upon him entirely unawares, and that his life's happiness would not be complete without her, *et cetera, et cetera*.

Mr. Stanwood didn't seem to be surprised. It was an old story to him. He swung around in his swivel chair and faced Mr. Wilbur, and thoughtfully looked him over. Mr. Wilbur submitted to the scrutiny gracefully, duly conscious that no eye, however discriminating, could detect a flaw in him. As a matter of fact, Mr. Stanwood rather liked Mr. Wilbur. He had known him for several years, and in all his wide acquaintance he didn't recall one individual whose coat set so well in the back. He would be a distinct addition to any family, would Mr. Wilbur.

"You haven't said anything to Marjorie about your—your regard for her, I assume?" Mr. Stanwood inquired at last.

"Nothing, of course," said Mr. Wilbur. "I didn't care to offer myself in a quarter where I might be objectionable."

"Quite right," commented Mr. Stanwood. "Lack of consideration for their elders is one of the besetting evils of the younger generation." There was a pause. "Have you any reason to believe that my daughter cares for you?" he asked at last.

Mr. Wilbur considered the matter thoughtfully in detail.

"I have dared to hope that I was not distasteful to her," he remarked at last. "My regard for her is such that I—I hope I can make her care for me."

"You know this thing of arbitrarily taking a young girl's happiness in hand is, I believe, a mistake in a great many cases," Mr. Stanwood observed didactically. "Don't you personally think it better to ascertain her wishes and desires before undertaking to guide them toward anyone object?"

"Yes, of course," Mr. Wilbur agreed. "I'm asking for permission to pay my attentions to your daughter. If I find I am not acceptable to her, except as a friend, I shall withdraw, of course."

A faint, luminous twinkle was in Mr. Stanwood's eyes.

"And if I say you may," he said after a moment, "I assume you are prepared to fight your own way with her? I am not to be called upon as arbiter. I shall neither employ coercion nor do anything to injure your chances. Personally, you are acceptable to me. I'll say that. She has the last choice, of course."

Mr. Wilbur arose, and in a burst of enthusiasm shook hands with Mr. Stanwood. There was a faint quaver of emotion in his voice when he spoke.

"Thank you, Mr. Stanwood," he said with an effort. "It's an honor that I scarcely dared to hope for."

Mr. Stanwood waved his gratitude aside.

"Don't thank me," he remarked. "You know you've got to settle with her yet. And now, Dan, how are you fixed financially? One must always have an eye on these things when one's own daughter is involved?"

Mr. Wilbur told him candidly, went into the possibilities of revamping the old family house in Eighty-first Street, and mentioned the chance of getting the Belknap cottage at Newport. Mr. Stanwood listened silently.

"Of course, all that's of no consequence," he said at the end. "Understand, Dan, that it's my daughter's happiness that is to be always considered." He was silent a little while. "And mere money isn't happiness, Dan," he said at last slowly. "No man knows that better than

I do." He shook off a sudden mood and came back to business again. "Dan, if you were left absolutely penniless, could you earn a living for your wife?" he asked. "After all, that is the main point."

"Really, Mr. Stanwood, the matter had never occurred to me in just that light before," Mr. Wilbur confessed falteringly. "I dare say I could, although there seems not even a remote possibility that I would ever have to do so."

"How could you, for instance?"

"Well—er—er—I should say I'd choose Wall Street."

"It takes money to start there," said Mr. Stanwood.

"Of course—I hadn't thought of that," Mr. Wilbur mused. "Well, there's a great deal to be made with a racing string, say," he went on hopefully.

Mr. Stanwood shook his head.

"More money to start," he said.

"Or—or—" And Mr. Wilbur was desperate. "I tell you," he burst out suddenly, "I could write a—a—book, say. I've been everywhere and done everything and seen everything, and they tell me some of these author chaps turn quite a penny at writing books."

Mr. Stanwood arose. It was a signal that the interview was at an end.

"Talk it over with Marjorie," he suggested kindly. "As I say, you're agreeable to me personally, but I shall use no influence either for or against. You understand?"

And while this was happening Lieutenant Faulkner was holding Marjorie Stanwood's hand and telling her that her heart line showed that she would marry only once, that she would love her husband devotedly—almost as much as he loved her—and that she would live to a ripe old age in perfect happiness.

XIV

C rabbed, crusty science tells us, encyclopedically, that electricity is our most potent force; wherefore it would appear that science is a musty, driveling, moth-eaten old dumbhead who never sat opposite a pair of brown eyes seeking potency. Electricity merely moves machinery, bridges illimitable space, and cures sciatica; while the power that lies in a woman's eyes makes the merry old world go 'round. It overturns empires, mocks at monarchs, bedevils diplomacy, and otherwise snarls things up through sheer lightness of heart. That is its amusement.

It's a science in itself, inexact if you please, and unfettered by known rules. But some day some chap will come along and make a serious study of it, and then, after five or ten or fifteen thousand years he will be competent to write a brief preface apologizing for scant information and general inaccuracies. All this power is there—particularly in brown eyes. They flicker and fleer, and promise and provoke, and flash and flame, and smolder and smother. Blue eyes are only brilliant, gray eyes are only gracious, black eyes are only bewitching, but brown eyes! Brown eyes are dangerous, if you please—yes, that's the word—dangerous!

It may be that that was the quality in Marjorie Stanwood's eyes which appealed to Lieutenant Faulkner. Danger! There is some popular tradition to the effect that the soldier delights in danger, and Lieutenant Faulkner was a soldier. All of which leads to the general conclusion that that fortune-telling episode may fairly be classed as an auspicious occasion. Holding a lady's hand for thirty-five minutes, and unfolding the unknown, with only an occasional hint of the obvious, is an achievement, for young hearts beat fast and ruddy blood leaps easily. Dan Wilbur would have considered it an impertinence; so would Marjorie Stanwood if Dan Wilbur had tried it.

Accustomed to material dangers and unawed by the intangible, Lieutenant Faulkner romped on the edge of the abyss and was smiling daringly into the brown eyes when finally Marjorie withdrew her hand.

"Yes, a long life and lots of happiness," he assured her glibly. "You'll never marry but once, and your husband'll be just crazy about you. He'll be a good fellow, your husband. I might even conjecture as to his—to his profession, if you are interested?"

Marjorie bit her red lips until they were redder than ever. And red lips, be it known, are just as dangerous as brown eyes—perhaps more so.

"Naturally I *am* interested," she said with a slight smile.

Lieutenant Faulkner drew a long breath and ceased smiling.

"You'll marry a—a—" and he paused. "I think you'd better let me examine your hand again." He reached for it.

Marjorie primly placed both hands behind her back.

"No," she said. "You've seen enough."

"But I can—I can do so much better when I'm looking at it," protested the lieutenant.

"I dare say," remarked Marjorie, but she didn't move her hands.

"Well," and the lieutenant thoughtfully stroked his chin, "I think, if I remember the lines of your hand well enough, I think perhaps you'll marry a—a—so—so—solemn looking chap with chin whiskers," he concluded desperately. "Really, you'd better let me look again," he blurted.

Marjorie shook her head and laughed outrageously for an instant—just an instant—while the red blood tingled in Lieutenant Faulkner's face. For the first time in his life he knew he was a coward—a quitter. He grinned sheepishly to cover his shame and went over to inspect some orchids on the table. Finally, he thrust an inquisitive nose into the brilliant, vapid blossoms, while Marjorie, with pensive eyes, critically examined the palm of her left hand. Neither had anything to say for a long time, and then:

"Who taught you to tell fortunes?" she asked calmly.

"A Spanish woman in the Philippines," he replied absently, without looking around. "She lived in a little ''dobe' hut on the outskirts of Cavite, a couple of miles from our camp."

"Young and pretty, I dare say?" she taunted.

"No, old, old, a regular old witch, who looked as if she might have kept a stable of broomsticks," returned the lieutenant. He was still staring at the orchids. "She had a dog named Alfonso XIII, so naturally all the Americans liked her; and she could *almost* cook a chicken *à la* Maryland," he added irrelevantly. "She was a bully old sport."

A faint suggestion of a smile curled the corners of Marjorie's red mouth. She was quite certain that no other man of her acquaintance would have stated the case just that way.

"And, of course, she told your fortune?" she inquired.

"Yes, lots of times," the lieutenant confessed. And he turned to face her with a singular gravity in his eyes. "And everytime she married me off to a different princess of Europe. You know she thought the United

States was just south of Switzerland, a sort of high C in the European concert." He was leaning against the table, watching her smile. "I like the Philippines," he added suddenly. "I've been thinking some of going back there—pretty soon?"

It was a question. The lieutenant was staring into brown eyes which met his unwaveringly; there came not one change in the curve of the scarlet lips; there was only the idlest interest in her manner. The lieutenant's eyes narrowed a little.

"She doesn't seem to have been very accurate in telling your fortune," Marjorie remarked carelessly. "At least, I dare say, you haven't married your princess yet?"

"Well, no," he confessed.

"And if she taught you, then *your* system can't be very good?"

"No, I suppose not," slowly.

Marjorie smoothed her skirt with one slender hand.

"I'm awfully glad," she said at last with a little sigh.

Lieutenant Faulkner took one impulsive step forward.

"Why?" he demanded eagerly. "Why?"

"I hate to think that I should ever have to marry a solemn looking chap with chin whiskers," replied Marjorie demurely. Then she laughed.

Lieutenant Faulkner didn't smile—the thing was past the smiling stage now—only stood looking at her with hands tightly clenched and infinite adoration in his eyes.

"I didn't dare say what I wanted to," he remarked steadily. "You know what I meant?" And he took *another* impulsive step forward. "It was—"

"Tell me something about the Philippines," interrupted Marjorie in a cooling, placid little voice. "I've never been there. Why do you want to go back?"

It was as good as a shower bath. The lieutenant stood tensely for an instant, then the fingers loosened their grip on his palms, and the declaration in his eyes was temporarily withdrawn. He sat down. He might just as well begin right now to educate her up to the army!

"Have you ever been to West Point?" he inquired.

"No."

"Or a garrison? Governor's Island?"

"No."

"It would be hard, then, for me to make you see just why I like the Philippines," he went on. "I think perhaps the real reason is that it's always possible for an enterprising young man," and he bowed modestly, "to get action out there—to start something. That appeals to me, and incidentally offers opportunities for advancement. Here in New York I'm idle; everybody's idle, and that isn't a man's work, you know." He was silent a moment. "If I had to stay here much longer I'd be wearing my handkerchief in my cuff."

Marjorie smiled slightly.

"Are you on furlough, then? A leave of absence? What would you call it?"

"No, not that—worse," replied the lieutenant hopelessly. "I'm attached to an advisory engineering board with nothing to do. It gets on my nerves. I'm positively oppressed by the desire to do something. The other night I chartered an automobile and skittered all over the landscape trying to make myself believe that something was happening." He paused and regarded Marjorie's profile gravely. "At West Point, you know, they only play at being soldiers, but you like it—the rigid discipline, and the grim way they do it; in a garrison there *are* soldiers, and you like them because they're the chaps we all depend upon even if they do seem to be idle; but in the Philippines, there's always work and lots of it, and it's worth while. Think of it! A handful of our men out there are holding uncounted millions of natives in the strait and narrow with their noses up to the tie-line, and they're busy every minute. If we ever give up the Philippines I'm going to resign from the army; there won't be anything left to do."

Now it just happened that Marjorie Stanwood didn't know another man in all the wide, wide world who worked for his living. Even papa only sat at a littered desk and told other men what to do, curtly, she thought. Of course *somebody* had to dig the ditches and mend the plumbing and sweep up the leaves in Central Park. And here was a young man who worked! The novelty of it was simply dazzling! And, further, he *liked* to work!

"It must be wonderful—the sense of responsibility, the work to be done," said Marjorie thoughtfully, dreamily.

"It *is* wonderful," the lieutenant agreed. "And it's not like anything you ever saw. A well-dressed woman walking along the principal street smoking an eight-inch cigar is liable to knock you a twister if you are not used to it; and they grow *flowers* out there—not odorless things like those," and he indicated the orchids. (He knew Dan Wilbur sent them.) "And sunsets! A sunset on Manila Bay is worth going around the world to see."

"I see—I can imagine," remarked Marjorie after a while, dreamily. "And you are going back. When?"

Lieutenant Faulkner had been dreaming a little. Something in the tone of her voice brought him back to earth and he regarded her thoughtfully.

"I don't know," he said. "I asked for my transfer a month ago. I'll get it, I know. It may come at anytime. It means at least two years there."

Marjorie arose and rearranged the orchids in the vase.

"Is New York absolutely intolerable to you?" she asked.

"It was getting so when I asked for the transfer," replied the lieutenant. "But in the last few days things have changed somewhat, and I'm—I'm not certain now that I want to go."

"Why?" It was a thin, far-away little voice.

Lieutenant Faulkner arose and went to her. She glanced up at him shyly, then her eyes dropped to the orchids again.

"Shall I really tell you?" he asked.

One white hand fluttered, and he reached for it eagerly.

"You *told* my fortune once, and I didn't—didn't like it very much," she said defensively, and the hand was withdrawn.

"Shall I *really* tell you?" he demanded again.

"No, *don't* tell me—*now*," she answered pleadingly. And she moved away a little.

"You know, don't you?"

"Yes, I know," faintly.

"And you?"

"It isn't *absolutely necessary* that you should go, is it?"

And just then Marjorie's maiden aunt, Miss Elvira Stanwood, entered the room.

XV

Lieutenant Faulkner never really hesitated but twice in his life—once on his first day in battle when he was introduced to the venomous *svutt* of a bullet which he knew was intended for him despite the fact that it was fired by an utter stranger, a man who could not possibly cherish any personal animosity against him; and again on that occasion when he laid his hand on the knob of the door leading into Mr. Stanwood's study. In each instance he advanced. He found the white-haired millionaire sitting at a huge rosewood desk. They had never met.

"Mr. Stanwood, I believe?" inquired the lieutenant.

"Yes."

"I am Lieutenant Faulkner."

Mr. Stanwood glanced at the card.

"Lieutenant Robert E. Lee Faulkner," he read. "Sit down."

Lieutenant Faulkner sat down. Mr. Stanwood turned to face him and favored him with one comprehensive sweep of his eyes.

"Of Virginia," Lieutenant Faulkner added. "Thirty years old, only son of General Putnam Faulkner, of the late Confederate States, a fighting man who, at least on one occasion, took the Federal forces over the high jumps; grandson of two Governors of Virginia in the days when public office was a patriotic obligation and not a commercial transaction; and direct descendant of Amenedab and Charity Faulkner, who landed at Jamestown about 1607 and were, respectively best man and matron of honor at the Pocahontas-John Rolfe nuptials."

Mr. Stanwood listened to this business-like statement with interest born of utter curiosity.

"Amenedab Faulkner, I may add, bore arms by warrant of the British Crown," Lieutenant Faulkner went on. "He was a great-grandson of a third son of a sword-maker of Birmingham who was knighted by the Crown in recognition of a very superior weapon he produced. I am the sole male survivor of the line, graduate of West Point, saw three years' active service in the Philippines with General Underwood, and Congress was kind enough to vote me a medal for services rendered. I have a mother and sister who live on a farm near Petersburg, Va."

Mr. Stanwood drew a long breath.

"It's interesting enough," he commented. "May I inquire the purpose of it all?"

Lieutenant Faulkner flowed steadily on.

"I am at present attached to an advisory engineering board here in New York, a sort of reward for long service in the field. So far as I am aware no member of my family has ever done a dishonorable thing, none was ever in jail, and none ever had enough money to keep him awake nights. I am a member of the Army and Navy Club, and in the course of another couple of years I believe I will be made a captain. For information as to my past performances I refer you to the Congress of the United States; as to my personal integrity, I refer you to the Secretary of War, or, nearer home, to General Underwood, also a member of the Army and Navy Club. I believe that covers the case."

He paused as if that were all. Mr. Stanwood was scrutinizing him carefully.

"What is the purpose of all this?" he asked again.

Lieutenant Faulkner drew a long breath.

"I have the honor to ask your daughter's hand in marriage," he explained steadily. "You didn't know me—I have introduced myself."

"Oh!" and the millionaire settled back in his chair with an expression which indicated faint amusement in his eyes. "Oh!" he said again. Had it not been that he was a little startled he probably would have laughed. Certainly he had never been approached in just this business-like manner before, and he fell to wondering what effect such a cyclonic young man must have had on Marjorie. And as he wondered a frown appeared on his brow.

"You take me unawares," he said after a moment, defensively. "Of course you know my daughter?"

"Very well indeed," the lieutenant boasted.

"And it so happens that I was not aware of your existence," said Mr. Stanwood. "I never even heard of you."

"I am only thirty," the lieutenant apologized.

There was something in his tone which caused Mr. Stanwood to pause deliberately and look him over again.

"How long have you known her—my daughter?" he inquired at last.

Lieutenant Faulkner blushed.

"Nearly a week," he said.

"Nearly a—!" The millionaire arose, amazed. He stared coldly down upon his caller for an instant with menacing eyes. "You haven't dared to intimate to her anything of—of affection, in so short a time?"

"I never intimate things," returned the lieutenant. "I told her I loved her, if that's what you mean?"

The jaws of the financial giant snapped viciously.

"And she, sir?" he thundered. "What did she say?"

"She said—er—I made her admit that she loved me," the lieutenant went on. "She told me, though, I was precipitate—headlong, I believe she said—but I explained that it would never happen again and she forgave even that."

"Headlong!" raved Mr. Stanwood. "I should say it *was* headlong!"

He stamped up and down his study violently. It was the first time in his life he had ever allowed himself to be surprised into anger. Lieutenant Faulkner was as placid as a summer sea; there was only a little steely glint in his eyes.

"Why, confound it, sir, it's unspeakable!" Mr. Stanwood bellowed in a rage. "You—you young—!"

"Epithets are utterly useless and not in the best of taste," the lieutenant cut in chillingly. "Sit down a moment."

And Mr. Stanwood sat down. To this day he wonders just what psychic force compelled so quick an obedience. And once in his chair he began to get control of himself again; the deadly, merciless calm which characterized every act of his life reasserted itself.

"I am amazed," he said at last.

"I gathered as much from your actions," observed the lieutenant. "Will you listen a moment?"

Mr. Stanwood stared at him mutely.

"I saw your daughter first at the opera," the lieutenant explained. "I was introduced to her at the Sanger ball and then and there I knew what my feelings were in the matter. I called on her in this house as any gentleman might have called. That I didn't meet you was unfortunate, of course, but I didn't. This afternoon I—I inadvertently told her I loved her."

"Inadvertently?" queried Mr. Stanwood.

"I mean it slipped out," the lieutenant explained. "I had intended to convince myself that my attentions would not be distasteful to her, and then I should have asked you for permission to pay my addresses. As it happened, a wheel slipped. Anyway, immediately I *did* know she cared for me I came straight to you." He paused a moment. "I fail to find any flaw in that course of conduct; certainly there is nothing to provoke epithets."

Mr. Stanwood wheeled in his chair and sat for a long time staring moodily out of the window. Lieutenant Faulkner merely waited.

"Young man, do you know what you are asking for?" he demanded at last as he turned.

"I do."

"And can you imagine how many men have made that same request?"

"It's a matter of no consequence."

"And the *position* of those men?" Mr. Stanwood went on emphatically. "Two dukes," he told them off on his fingers, "one earl, three marquises, and half a dozen counts."

"Charity forbids me making any comment upon the foreign noblemen who come to this country to woo the daughter of one of the richest men in the United States," the lieutenant remarked evenly. "Your question answers itself—your daughter is still unmarried."

Mr. Stanwood blinked a little.

"She could marry today practically any man in this country," he went on, almost apologetically, "no matter what his wealth or position."

"The greater the compliment to me," the lieutenant urged. "She *loves* me!"

"Hang it, that's what's the matter," the millionaire flamed suddenly. "No other man would have dared to do what you have done—go to my daughter first. You haven't played the game as they played it."

"That's why I'm here," returned the lieutenant calmly. He leaned back in his chair and clasped his hands around one knee. "*You* didn't play the *financial* game as others played it; that's why *you* are here."

It took Mr. Stanwood a minute to get that, and having it it was a tremendous thing to think about. He thought about it a long time. It had a tremendously placating influence. Finally, he favored the lieutenant with one sidelong glance, and fussed with some papers on his desk.

"I suppose," he said with dangerous deliberation, "you consider yourself perfectly able to take care of a wife?"

Lieutenant Faulkner's heart leaped.

"I do," he said firmly.

"And what, may I inquire, is your income?"

"Eighteen hundred dollars a year!"

"Eighteen hundred dollars a—!" And Mr. Stanwood was on his feet raving again. "Eighteen hundred dollars a year!" he repeated. "Why, confound it, sir, my butler makes more than that."

"Any other man may if he is sufficiently lacking in self-respect," remarked the lieutenant.

The millionaire was facing him with clenched fists and blazing eyes.

"Your confounded impertinence—" he raged. "Do you know what it costs to *run this house?* One thousand dollars a day, sir. How far could you go with that?"

The lieutenant glanced about the sumptuous apartment.

"I'm afraid it wouldn't be much longer than three o'clock tomorrow afternoon," he remarked, and he arose. "I think I understand," he added. "You prefer to make your daughter's marriage a financial proposition?"

Mr. Stanwood grew suddenly dangerously calm.

"There is nothing further to be said," he went on. "The thing is utterly preposterous." He indicated the door with a sweep of his hand.

"Before I go I'll just add that I came to you as a personal favor to *you*," Lieutenant Faulkner said slowly. "I wanted to feel that I had complied with the conventions. When one does that one's self-respect is flattered."

"Personal favor to me," Mr. Stanwood repeated. "And please do me another. Don't ever call here again."

"I never shall—until you invite me," replied Lieutenant Faulkner.

XVI

(Being a literal report of a conversation over the telephone between Mr. Fulton Stanwood, millionaire, and General Underwood, U. S. A.)

H ello!"
      "Hello! That General Underwood?"

"Yes."

"I'm Mr. Stanwood—Mr. Fulton Stanwood, of Wall Street."

"Well?"

"Who in the hell is this Lieutenant Robert E. Lee Faulkner?"

"Who in the hell do you think you are talking to?"

"This is General Underwood, isn't it?"

"Yes, not a flunkey, as you evidently imagine."

"Well, I'm Mr. Fulton Stanwood, of Wall Street, and—"

"I don't care if you're Crœsus. Don't talk to me like that. What do you want?"

(Pause.)

"I beg your pardon. I'm afraid I was a little abrupt."

"*Afraid* you were abrupt? You know damned *well* you were abrupt. What do you want?"

(Pause.)

"I would like to inquire, please, as to Lieutenant Faulkner's character and standing?"

"He's a gentleman and a soldier, sir. And he wouldn't have called me away from a game of bridge to ask idiotic questions."

"I mean, what's he ever done? What are his family connections? What are his prospects?"

"He's done more than any other man of his age in the army, and Congress voted him a medal for personal gallantry; his family connections are a great deal better than those of any other man I know; and he will be commander-in-chief of the army of the United States if he lives long enough."

(Pause.)

"Unmarried, I suppose?"

"Yes, and consequently happy."

"Is he the sort of man to whom you would give your daughter?"

"My *daughter*! Confound you, I'm a bachelor. But if I had a daughter I'd hand her to him on a gold platter."

(Pause.)

"His relations with you, I dare say, are rather cordial?"

"Cordial? He's an impertinent young shave tail, sir. He's the only man living who ever called me down in the field. That all?"

"I—think—that's—all."

(Pause.)

"Did you say anything?"

"No—I—was—just—thinking that—"

"Excuse me. I thought you said 'Thank you.'" (Bang!)

(Bang!)

XVII

We will now rhapsodize a few lines about the Baize Curtains. The dictionary says that baize is a "sort of coarse, woolen stuff." These were not that kind of Baize Curtains. These Baize Curtains, of an unromantic gray green, were, by reflected glory, at once a cloth of gold, and hangings of royal purple, and attar scented fine linen. They were the gossamer shield behind which Love hid; the tantalizing draperies which Cupid drew against the prying eyes of the world; the roseate lining of a den where hand might meet hand in one clinging, thrilling touch, while the voice of the sordid earth grew vague and faint; the completing wall of a nook of delight whereof the furnishings were two chairs, a wobbly table, sparkling cut glass and silver, and spotless napery. And, lo! the Lord of the Baize Curtains was the waiter; and even *he* always said "Ahem!" before he ventured to draw them.

The Baize Curtains hung down as straight and uncompromisingly as a pair of oaken boards, cutting off a many windowed little room which grows fungus-like, straight out from the east wall of the dining room of the Casino in Central Park. In the large room, always quiet, there is, nevertheless, the publicity of Sherry's or Delmonico's, but in the nook behind the Baize Curtains is a haven and a refuge. Only the eyes of the waiter come here, and a discreet waiter can neither see nor hear.

The large room was deserted save for one person—a gentleman in an automobile coat. His leather cap lay on a chair beside him, and he was gazing reflectively into the depths of an amber colored, iced liquid on the table in front of him. The sun was slowly dropping down off there somewhere behind Central Park West, and a crimson glow was creeping into the room. The gentleman was Dan Wilbur. He was mooning over that scene in the play where John Drew came right out and told the girl he loved her. It had seemed so easy, so necessary, so natural, so politely impetuous. And he wondered what Marjorie had thought of it.

His sentimental meditations were disturbed by a laugh, a suppressed gurgle of merriment which caused him to turn and stare inquiringly at the Baize Curtains, inscrutable as the face of Fate. He was still staring fixedly when the laughter came again, this time a little louder, and then a woman, hidden in the recess, spoke:

"No, no, no!" she declared positively. "That would never do."

A man's voice mumbled something that he didn't catch, and then the woman spoke again:

"Why, that's too prosaic. Since it is going to be an elopement, and all our plans are made, let's make it just as romantic as possible. Won't it be just too delicious?"

Mr. Wilbur's eyes were no longer listening—they were startled as he sat staring at the curtain. His moodiness passed, and he was suddenly, keenly, alertly alive. The voice! There was never another in the world quite like it; it stirred every quiescent faculty into activity, and his hands closed spasmodically. An elopement! Our plans!

The man mumbled something else.

"Think of it!" the woman exclaimed, and she laughed again. "I'd give a thousand dollars to see his face when he knows it."

Mr. Wilbur *knew* that voice now, knew it beyond all possible mistake, and some quick, subtle working of his mind brought hard lines into his face. He was not an eavesdropper, but it never occurred to him for one instant to relax his attention to the conversation behind the Baize Curtains. Once he made as if to arise, but he dropped back again; a silent-shod waiter glanced in at the door. Mr. Wilbur waved him away and still sat listening.

"He can't have the faintest idea of it, of course," said the woman after another little pause. "How long will it take us to get there?"

Mr. Wilbur strained his ears vainly to get the answer. It was only a mumble.

"What time is it now?" the woman asked again.

Mr. Wilbur glanced at his watch. It was twenty minutes past six o'clock.

"We'd better be going, then," suggested the woman.

Mr. Wilbur heard the rustle of silken skirts, and involuntarily picked up a newspaper to shield himself, then:

"You dear, *dear, dear*! Of course I love you, silly." Then, impetuously, passionately: "I love you more than anything else in all the world. You know it, don't you?" And then: "But I'm just so excited about this that—that I can't hold myself. Yes, just one."

And then—and *then*—! Mr. Wilbur's modest ears were shocked by the unmistakable sound of a—a *kiss*! Yes, it was a kiss! He heard a chair pushed back, and a moment later a woman parted the Baize Curtains; a man appeared just behind her. A reddened ray of the dying sun illuminated them both for an instant, and Mr. Wilbur's teeth closed involuntarily as he dodged behind his newspaper.

The woman was Susan, and the man a black-mustached, business-like individual, square and soldierly from the tips of his boots to the top of his black head, with a keen, determined face and shrewd, penetrating eyes. It was the man Mr. Wilbur had met going into the apartment house where Susan lived.

They passed Mr. Wilbur and went out.

XVIII

So deep was Mr. Wilbur's abstraction when he left the Casino that he only gave the waiter half a dollar instead of a dollar, his usual tip. He cranked up thoughtfully, the spark caught, and the huge, high-power machine began churning restlessly. Mr. Wilbur stood staring at the polished sides blankly for a time, then pulled his leather cap down tight, clambered in, and slid slowly down the incline to the driveway below. He turned north, not for any particular reason—merely because it happened so.

Susan! An elopement! It had come to this! That dark-mustached chap—he knew him perfectly! And Susan *did* kiss him! Every act of hers since his return passed before him in review. It was obvious—pitifully, vulgarly obvious! A jealous husband, the unremitting attentions of another man, tawdry flattery, clandestine meetings and letters, perhaps, the final triumph of a senseless infatuation, and now—now this hideous thing! It always happened so. And yet, it was beyond belief. He himself couldn't have believed it if he had not known the circumstances so well, from Susan's own red lips, and heard—*actually heard*—what had happened behind the Baize Curtains.

Gradually a sense of his own responsibility in the affair began to take possession of him. Perhaps it would have been better had he suddenly discovered himself to them there in the dining room. He had read somewhere in a book of a woman who had been turned back from a fatal mistake by the timely appearance of a friend. As it was, he had been passed unrecognized—they had seen only the back of his newspaper. If he had made himself known and had allowed just a word to drop, showing that he knew all, it might have altered everything. The more he thought of it in this light the more he blamed himself, and now—and now he was helpless. He had blunderingly let the opportunity pass.

Mr. Wilbur loosened his speed clutch, sighed a little, and went skimming along the East Drive. Through the rapidly deepening shadows, somewhere opposite One Hundredth Street, Mr. Wilbur saw the glint of a tail light ahead and slowed up a little. As he did so the car in front swerved erratically, ran clear of the road, and butted into a tree. There it stopped, restlessly battering its hood to bits. He heard a slight feminine scream, and some vigorous man-talk, whereupon he stopped his car, leaped out, and ran across to the other car.

Just as he reached it a woman jumped out. It was Susan! And then came an awful moment. Susan recognized him instantly, and opened her mouth helplessly, then she glanced suddenly at her companion, and couldn't think of a word to say. Dan Wilbur and her husband—her *real* husband—face to face at last! Her first mad idea was ignominious flight, her second tears, her third screams; but finally, she decided that the only thing to do was to faint. It would at least give her time to get her bearings; and she hoped it wouldn't mess up her skirt. So she fainted. No one had expected it, and she tumbled down in an undignified heap in the middle of the road.

"What made her do that?" demanded the dark-mustached man in astonishment.

"I imagine she's hurt," said Mr. Wilbur sharply.

"Why, she couldn't have been hurt," protested the dark-mustached man. "Nothing but a little jolt—we were barely moving."

Together they leaned over Susan, and Susan's husband—Lieutenant Paul Abercrombie Harwell Rowland—raised the inert body and rested her head against his knee. A hairpin gave her an awful jab in the head, but she couldn't afford even to moan.

"Scared, that's all," he explained tersely. "Get me a capful of water out of the tank there."

There was no if-you-please or will-you-kindly in this man's manner of speaking. Mr. Wilbur obeyed mechanically, albeit hurriedly. There was a certain grim triumph in all this, for had not Fate handed Susan over to him to save from her own folly? It was Providence, he was certain of it. After they revived her—then—then!

The two men worked heroically over Susan. They splashed water in the pretty, still face, and mussed up the radiant, sunshiny hair, and chafed the delicate hands, and finally Paul slapped her rosy cheeks sharply. It was the army method. Mr. Wilbur was about to protest at the unnecessary vigor of this treatment when he happened to glance up and found that every vehicle north of Fourteenth Street seemed to have stopped, hedging them in, and there were a dozen offers of assistance.

Paul disregarded them all, working steadily on. Susan positively declined to be revived. Finally, something of apprehension came into Paul's manner. The shock must have been greater than he imagined. He glanced up and around at the crowd.

"Is there a physician here?" he queried shortly.

No answer.

"We'll have to get her to a doctor," Paul told Dan Wilbur hurriedly. "I'm afraid it's something serious after all." And it *was*! "My steering gear seems to be out of commission. Will you give us a lift?"

Fate was dealing the trump hand to Dan Wilbur, as he saw it.

"Certainly," he responded quickly. "I know a doctor chap over here in Ninety-sixth Street—be there in two minutes."

Susan was lifted into the tonneau of Mr. Wilbur's car. Paul climbed in beside her, and sat supporting the slender, graceful figure in his arms. Mr. Wilbur scrambled into the front seat.

"Open up there ahead," he bawled.

The huge car trembled, moved, and rushed away. When it stopped in Ninety-sixth Street, Paul gathered up Susan in his strong arms and carried her up the steps and into the physician's office. She was laid upon a couch, and the gray-bearded old medicine man made a cursory examination, Paul and Dan Wilbur looking on. Mr. Wilbur was planning his course of procedure.

"If you gentlemen will wait in the reception room?" the doctor suggested.

"Is it serious?" Paul demanded anxiously.

"Doesn't seem to be," was the reply. "Step outside."

He held open the door as they passed out, and closed it behind them, after which he turned back to his patient. Susan suddenly sat up perfectly straight on the couch, with flushed face and disheveled hair.

"Have they gone?" she queried breathlessly.

Dr. Graybeard tugged at his whiskers in thoughtful surprise.

"Only outside," he said at last. "Can I do anything for you, madam?"

"Just let me think! Let me think!" exclaimed Susan.

The physician aimlessly stirred up a mixture of aromatic spirits of ammonia while Susan thought. After a while there came a sharp rap on the door, and Paul threw it open.

"Paul, Paul!" Susan exclaimed, and she extended her arms to him. "Where is *he*?"

"*He*?" Paul repeated. "Oh! the other chap. I was afraid to leave you, and to prevent delay I sent him in his automobile to pick up the girl. He's to meet you and me and Faulk at the preacher's in Sixty-fifth Street just as soon as he can get there."

Susan was staring at him in wild-eyed horror.

"You sent *him* to bring Mar—" she began stammeringly. "Paul Rowland, *don't—you—know—who—that—man—was?*"

"No. Seemed to be all right. Why?"

"Why that was *Dan Wilbur!*"

Then Susan *really* fainted.

XIX

That little interview between Dan Wilbur and Lieutenant Paul Abercrombie Harwell Rowland in the physician's reception room had been pithy and pointed and pertinent. Paul had all sorts of trouble on his mind, among them a fainting wife, possibly hurt, and the sole direction of the destiny of two trusting hearts. He paced back and forth across the room, watch in hand, the while Mr. Wilbur regarded him coldly, conscious that he was the instrument of Fate in this thing. Mr. Wilbur had just opened his listless mouth to give voice to a diplomatic catapult when Paul turned on him suddenly.

"I say, old man," he complained, "we're in all sorts of a hole."

By "we" Mr. Wilbur understood that he included Susan in the next room. He retired the diplomatic catapult to await orders; perhaps this fellow would commit himself.

"In what way?" Mr. Wilbur inquired frigidly.

Paul was staring at him hard.

"You know circumstances occasionally arise when it is not only inadvisable for gentlemen to know each other, but it would be the height of indiscretion for them to introduce themselves," Paul went on evenly. "Now I don't happen to know your name, and you don't know mine. I only know that you gave prompt and willing assistance when we needed it, and I thank you for it."

Mr. Wilbur waved his hand deprecatingly.

"Now I'm going to ask a favor of you," Paul continued. "If it is within your power to grant it I hope you will; and if you do it will instantly make it indiscreet for me to know you and you to know me, at least for the present. Frankly, if you do it and get away with it, it's going to kick up a dickens of a row, and in that event the less you know about me and the less I know about you the better."

Mr. Wilbur was getting interested. By Jove, it was just like a page out of a Williamson story, mixed up with an Agnes and Egerton Castle chapter.

"Coming down to brass tacks, there's an elopement on," Paul continued, still staring hard at Mr. Wilbur. "We were to go meet the girl at a quarter of seven o'clock. It's now about five minutes past seven, and—" He waved his hands despairingly.

"This—this—" and Mr. Wilbur nodded toward the other room, "this isn't the girl then?"

JACQUES FUTRELLE

"No," Paul replied. "My—er—this lady has nothing to do with the affair beyond chaperoning the girl to the place of meeting." He paused. "My car is somewhere in the park, out of commission; I can't go away and leave *her* here not knowing what's the matter with her; it's twenty minutes past meeting time, and the bride-to-be is probably crying her eyes out. Your car is at the door. You can straighten the whole thing out. Will you do it?"

And then a huge wave of comprehension swept over Mr. Wilbur. Susan was *not* eloping! Of course not! She was merely aiding someone who was. Perhaps this black-mustached chap was the bridegroom!

"Will you do it?" Paul repeated tersely.

Nothing so quickly begets a spirit of reparation as a realization of having wronged one. Suddenly Mr. Wilbur found himself utterly ashamed of his suspicions, and with this shame came an irresistible impulse to make amends by whatever means came to hand. Here evidently was an opportunity to oblige Susan.

"I'll do it," he said unhesitatingly. "Where am I to go?"

"One other thing," Paul continued impressively. "It may be, if the girl is still waiting, there will be an attempt made to follow you. Of course you would know what to do in that case?"

"I understand," replied Mr. Wilbur.

He drew out a pair of goggles and tied them on, settled his cap, tugged at his gloves, and accepted a card which Paul handed him. There were some crisp instructions and he went out. Paul stood still until he heard the whirr of the automobile outside as it started away, and then went in to tell Susan.

Mr. Wilbur pulled out of Ninety-sixth Street into Central Park West and went due north with slowly increasing momentum. The wind brushed his cheeks gratefully and fanned a smoldering enthusiasm into flames. It was the nearest thing to an adventure that had ever come his way. And he was beginning to like it tremendously. The uncertainty of it all, and the mystery, and the feeling of responsibility for the happiness of two unknown hearts! Confound it, it was bully to be doing something. Fortunately for his peace of mind it did not occur to him that he had heard Susan kiss this dark-mustached chap, and avow her love for him—he remembered only that he had misjudged her and that now he was making amends.

At One Hundred and Fifth Street a policeman shouted at him warningly. Mr. Wilbur grinned with the sheer delight of the thing and slithered on his way. He turned east at One Hundred and Tenth Street with undiminished speed, and the north end of Central Park slid gloomily past on his right. At St. Nicholas Avenue he eased up a little and proceeded more sedately to Fifth Avenue. A few quick, furtive glances all around, then he turned and came back along One Hundred and Tenth Street very slowly, hugging the curb next to the Park, until he had covered about half a block. There he stopped.

"Honk, honk, honk!" remarked the car impatiently. Then: "Honk, honk!" And again: "Honk, honk!"

Mr. Wilbur peered with eager eyes into the darkness. After a moment a figure detached itself from the shadows—a slender girlish figure—and ran toward the automobile. Mr. Wilbur leaped out and threw open the door of the tonneau, incidentally straining his eyes to get a glimpse of the girl's face as he handed her in. His curiosity was rebuked by a heavy veil which enviously enveloped head and face and throat. But Mr. Wilbur knew intuitively that she was pretty.

He paused for just a moment to satisfy himself that his machine was shipshape, and then with a feeling of exultation took his seat again. A veiled lady! By George, it was all according to Hoyle! The accident in the park, the mysterious man, and the veiled lady! The car moved west slowly. He almost regretted that the only thing remaining for him to do now was to deliver the girl to an address in Sixty-fifth Street—the number written on the card. Anyway he would claim the right of being best man at the wedding!

His meditations were interrupted by the weight of a light hand on his shoulder. He turned suddenly.

"Look!" exclaimed the veiled lady anxiously.

Mr. Wilbur looked. A huge touring car had bulged suddenly into the street from Fifth Avenue, and was drawing up at the curb on the park side. It contained a chauffeur, one other man, and a woman in the rear seat.

"Honk, honk, honk!" said the newcomer. "Honk, honk!" And again: "Honk, honk!"

"The signal, by Jove!" remarked Mr. Wilbur to himself. "It isn't all over after all." And he was positively glad of it.

"Honk, honk, honk!" his car bellowed defiantly. "Honk, honk!" And again: "Honk, honk!"

It was a spirit of dare-deviltry that prompted him. Instantly the challenge was accepted, and the big touring car behind started forward with a jerk. Mr. Wilbur grinned, kicked loose the speed clutch and started west in earnest.

"Honk, honk, honk!" screamed the car behind. It was moving like the wind now.

"Honk, honk, honk!" taunted the car ahead.

Speed ordinances are idiotic things, anyway. If you don't believe it ask any automobilist. Mr. Wilbur didn't think much of them evidently, for he gave his car her head now, and buckled down over the steering wheel. He glanced back once to reassure the veiled lady.

"Don't be alarmed," he said exultantly. "Nothing on wheels can catch this car."

Straight along One Hundred and Tenth Street, then a sudden swerve to the right, and St. Nicholas Avenue lay straight before him. The other car came on and swerved in after him. Delightful little thrills were chasing up and down Mr. Wilbur's aristocratic spine. He would keep going uptown until he shook off his pursuer, then dodge out of the way and double back. That was his purpose; and incidentally it was one of the few times in his life that he had a definite purpose.

And so the cars raced on, sworn at by pedestrians, shouted at by policemen, barked at by little dogs until Central Park was lost in the darkness behind, and they were both swallowed up in the wilds of Harlem.

XX

While telephone, telegraph, special messengers, and two private detectives were busily ransacking New York City for Mr. Stanwood, he was sitting in the drawing-room of his country place at Tarrytown, on a Chippendale settle with his feet on a Louis XIV chair, telling Mortimer how to hang a picture. The place hadn't been opened for the season, the 'phones had not been connected, therefore it was the most unlikely place for Mr. Stanwood to be.

"A little more to the right, Mortimer," he directed.

"Yes, sir."

And just then Hollis came in.

"Please, sir, Mr. Wilbur is here," Hollis announced, "and is very anxious to see you immediately."

"Dan Wilbur?" inquired Mr. Stanwood. "Tell him to come in."

And a moment later Dan Wilbur appeared. Beneath a coating of dust Mr. Stanwood was able to recognize him, and he arose in surprise.

"What's the matter, Dan?" he inquired. "Sit down."

"I haven't a moment," Mr. Wilbur apologized. "I didn't know you were up here. I came by on a chance of being able to borrow a car from your garage. I knew you kept one or two up here. May I have it?"

"Certainly," replied Mr. Stanwood. "But what's the matter? What's the excitement?"

"My machine broke down a couple of hundred yards back here," Mr. Wilbur explained hastily. "I must have another at once in order to—to get back to New York. It's a matter of vital importance." He paused thoughtfully. "There's another car behind, chasing me."

"Chasing you?" repeated Mr. Stanwood. "Hollis, run around to the garage and bring that sixty-horse power machine to the door." Then, to Mr. Wilbur: "Who's chasing you? And why?"

Mr. Wilbur nervously removed his goggles and tied them on again.

"Well, as a matter of fact," he confessed, "I'm mixed up in an elopement, and—"

"Elopement?" interrupted Mr. Stanwood in amazement. "Elopement?"

"Oh, *I'm* not eloping," Mr. Wilbur hastened to explain. "I'm helping a chap who was to meet the girl and take her to the place to be married. Immediately after I picked her up this other car appeared in pursuit, and we've been racing all over Westchester ever since. My idea, of course, was to dodge them and get back to New York, then just as I lost sight of them my car broke down. I hid the girl out in the woods a couple of hundred yards back here until I could come here and borrow a car. That's all. She's waiting, scared to death, I suppose, out there in the woods, and I don't happen to know how far back the pursuing car is."

He stopped breathlessly. There was a twinkle in Mr. Stanwood's eyes.

"If you're violating no confidence, who is the girl?" he asked.

Mr. Wilbur stared at him blankly.

"I don't know," he confessed. "I don't even know who the man is. I don't know anything about it, except that I'm honor bound to shake off that other car and get her down to Sixty-fifth Street in a hurry."

Mr. Stanwood laughed outright.

"Why, confound it, you've stirred up a genuine adventure, haven't you?" he chuckled. He clapped Mr. Wilbur on the shoulder and led him toward the front door. "I didn't think it was in you, Dan," he added.

"'Tis kind of queer, isn't it?" Mr. Wilbur said. "I rather liked it at first—something different, you know. But I couldn't lose that car behind me to save me. There must be a thousand dollars in fines piled up against my machine. Every policeman I passed shouted at me, and took my number."

"Not getting tired of it, Dan?" Mr. Stanwood rebuked. "And you haven't delivered the girl yet! Think of the anxious hearts that are awaiting her. Say, Dan," he went on suddenly, "let me get in, won't you? I haven't had any real excitement for ten years. Let me go along with you? I'm going back to the city, anyway."

Mr. Wilbur considered it thoughtfully.

"I can't see any objection," he said at last. "The girl won't mind, I don't suppose. I'm going to cut for the city as soon as I get the car. Come along."

The churning of Mr. Stanwood's automobile came to them faintly from outside. The millionaire swooped up hat and coat and rushed out, following Mr. Wilbur. They routed out Hollis and tumbled into the front seat, side by side. In the bow of his own automobile, Mr. Stanwood instantly assumed command.

"Now, let's get the girl," he directed tersely, "and then, Dan, my boy, we'll show 'em just how good we are. We two are equal to an army, eh?"

He poked Mr. Wilbur jovially in the ribs and chuckled. Why this was more fun than he'd ever had before in all his life!

"Of course if that other automobile doesn't come along it's simple enough now," Mr. Wilbur explained as he put on power.

"Let her come," boasted Mr. Stanwood. "We'll run the legs off her."

Under Mr. Wilbur's dexterous manipulation the car twisted and squirmed out into the road again, and went snooping along through the darkness. After a minute or so the lights of his own car, stationary beside the road, rose out of the gloom and he stopped beside it.

"Honk, honk, honk!" observed the new car blatantly. "Honk, honk!" And again: "Honk, honk!"

There was a crackling of twigs in the underbrush to the left, and the veiled lady appeared timidly, silhouetted against the light. Mr. Stanwood gallantly leaped out. For an instant the veiled lady hesitated as Mr. Stanwood approached, hesitated as if contemplating flight.

"It's all right—I'm here," Mr. Wilbur called out.

"Here we are—right in here," Mr. Stanwood instructed. "Got a little new blood in the game, that's all," and he handed her into the tonneau. "Now don't worry for a moment, little lady," he added paternally. "We'll pull you through all right. 'All the world loves a lover,' you know. Ha! ha! ha! We won't keep him waiting a minute longer than we can possibly help."

The veiled lady shrank back timidly into the farthest corner before this good-natured outburst of assurance; and, still chuckling, Mr. Stanwood clambered in beside Mr. Wilbur again. Mr. Wilbur was listening intently, and Mr. Stanwood also listened. Faintly there came to them the *chug-chug-chug* of a rapidly moving car, and as they all looked back her dazzling lights flashed into sight around a curve in the roadway.

"*There* she comes!" announced Mr. Stanwood delightedly.

"*Here* we go!" announced Mr. Wilbur grimly.

"Now, my boy," remarked Mr. Stanwood placidly, "let's show 'em how fast a *real* automobile can run."

Mr. Wilbur pulled her wide open, and the machine fairly jumped out of her tracks. Mr. Stanwood's hat went skimming off into the night like a rifle shot, and he only laughed.

"Honk, honk, honk!" bleated the pursuing car.

"Honk, honk, honk!" Mr. Stanwood bleated back at it.

The wind was sweeping up into their faces, the keen night air was stinging color into their cheeks, and Mr. Stanwood's hatless white head looked like a venerable porcupine. He settled back comfortably, enjoying every instant of it, while the darkened world went reeling past.

JACQUES FUTRELLE

XXI

Mr. Wilbur's was a master hand on the steering wheel. Mr. Stanwood looked on admiringly at the ease and certainty with which he held sixty horse power at his finger tips, the while he permitted himself to vaguely regret that such a blamed good chauffeur had been spoiled to make only a tamely interesting man of the world. However, if he got Dan in the family that would be something. Which reminded him of the surpassing impertinence of the impecunious Lieutenant Faulkner. Eighteen hundred a year! Confound him!

For half a mile or so the cars slid on through the night seemingly without the variation of a hair's breadth in their position, each to the other.

"Can't you give her some more power?" Mr. Stanwood shouted in Mr. Wilbur's ear.

"I'm using every pound she's got," Mr. Wilbur shouted back.

"That chap back there's sticking like glue," Mr. Stanwood bawled. And that chap back there could drive a car, *too*, if anybody asked about it. Henri, his own chauffeur, didn't have a thing on that chap back there.

And then slowly, slowly, they began to draw away from the pursuing car. Their advantage was almost imperceptible at first, but after a minute or so the pursuer's lights began to drop back rapidly, and the clamor of her engines grew fainter. A lucky bend in the road hid the dazzling eyes behind for an instant, and Mr. Wilbur availed himself of this to twist off suddenly to the right, along an intersecting road. A few hundred yards that way and he turned again to the right, doubled back and crossed their own track, coming out at last on a spider web of road. The hound-like car behind was shaken off, at least temporarily.

"Maybe that wasn't all right?" bellowed Mr. Stanwood enthusiastically. "Now, cut it for New York."

Mr. Wilbur eased up slightly.

"You don't know that chap back there," he remarked. "I've lost him two or three times, but he always turns up again. He's a mind reader."

"Well, if we can keep out of his sight until we get back to town he's lost all right," said Mr. Stanwood conclusively. "Go 'way off on the west side and we'll make our grandstand finish down Riverside Drive. And don't slow up." He turned to the veiled lady in the rear. "We're all right now," he assured her.

She nodded graciously.

Now, Mr. Wilbur was not the sort of a man to keep two fond hearts in suspense, so he gave the car her head again. He hadn't the faintest idea what time it was, but it must be at least an hour and a half since he started. That dark-mustached chap and Susan must be thinking all sorts of things. Of course they would understand that something had happened, because the dark-mustached chap had intimated that—

Suddenly a man stepped out into the roadway in front of them and waved his arms frantically. Confound it. Here was another fine to be charged up to his car. No, it wasn't his car, after all. It was Mr. Stanwood's car. Mr. Wilbur grinned a little and went skidding over to the left, intending to pass this human semaphore. But this particular human semaphore evidently anticipated something of this kind, as there had been no diminution of speed, so he made a megaphone of his hands and bawled at them:

"Bridge—down—ahead!"

"What!" exclaimed Mr. Wilbur.

Click! And the churning of the engines ceased. Snap! And the brake was on, gently at first, then harder, until the hurtling car came to a standstill with a groan a couple of hundred feet farther on. The human semaphore was strolling toward them. Mr. Stanwood and Mr. Wilbur leaped out and went back to meet him.

"Did you say there was a bridge down?" Mr. Wilbur inquired briskly. "Where is it?"

The man regarded him with a smile of complete superiority.

"I don't know," he answered. "Just a little trick of mine to stop you chaffers when you're speeding. It always gets 'em the first time I work it on 'em. You gents'll have to come along to the police station."

Mr. Stanwood and Mr. Wilbur stared at the plain clothes man for one mute instant, and then Mr. Stanwood arose and declared himself. Hot, passionate, sizzling words flowed from his lips in a torrent; plain and fancy expletives, ground and lofty adjectives, and verbal flip-flops, added to which was a heterogeneous mass of just ordinary American cuss words. Contemptible little rat! A trick like that when they were in a hurry!

The plain clothes man listened to the end complacently, making a mental note of some of the words which were new to him. He drew a long breath at the finish.

"That makes two charges," he said at last. "Speeding and profanity."

That started Mr. Stanwood going again, but Mr. Wilbur laid a restraining hand on his arm and he simmered down.

"Now look here," said Mr. Stanwood, "it's out of the question for us to go with you. We have—er—a lady in the car, and we must get down town at once. We understand your position, of course. There's no one around, and I think perhaps I have a fifty-dollar bill here that might be useful to you?"

"That makes attempted bribery," remarked the plain clothes man. "Speeding, profanity, and attempted bribery."

And then Mr. Stanwood *did* blow up.

"Why, confound you," he blazed, "if you keep adding up those things against me like that I'll—I'll give you a poke in the nose."

"*And* threatening an officer," supplemented the incorruptible one. "There ain't anything to it—you gents'll have to go with me."

Compared to what Mr. Stanwood said now, the things he had said previously were mere idle fripperies, lightsome repartee, airy persiflage, decorative rhetoric, colorless colloquialisms. He kept saying them until he ran down, the while Mr. Wilbur, from time to time, gazed off into the darkness behind apprehensively. This elopement, according to Susan's plans and specifications, seemed to be in a bad way; and if that other car should happen to turn up again!

"Let me speak to the gentleman," remarked Mr. Wilbur at last. He took the plain clothes man by the arm and purred into a large, red ear. "Now, Mister—Mister—may I inquire your name, sir?"

"Jenkins," the officer obliged.

"Jenkins!" repeated Mr. Wilbur in amazement. "Why," and he seized one of the officer's hands and shook it effusively, "why, you must be a son of old man Jenkins, then, aren't you?"

Mr. Jenkins feebly admitted that he was.

"Why, think of it!" Mr. Wilbur rippled on smoothly. "Running across you like this! Why, I feel as if I'd known you always—heard so much about you and all that." He drew back and peered into the other's face. "Just like your father, too," he complimented. "Say, now, old chap, you and I can understand each other in just a minute."

Mr. Jenkins wasn't so certain about it; however, he didn't say anything. Mr. Wilbur leaned forward again and buzzed in his ear.

"You see," he confessed, "it's an elopement. The lady's in the automobile there, and her folks are in a car behind chasing us. If they catch us it's all off. Do you see?"

"Where did you know my father?" Mr. Jenkins inquired suspiciously.

Mr. Wilbur buzzed on hastily:

"Two blighted hearts, and all that sort of thing, you know. You are going to let us pass—I know you are. Ha! ha! ha! It will be a good joke to tell your father, eh? Held up one of his oldest friends, as he was eloping."

"Where did you know my father?" Mr. Jenkins insisted again.

Mr. Wilbur's mind went utterly blank. He turned helplessly to Mr. Stanwood.

"Where was it we met Mr. Jenkins, father?" he inquired. "In—er—oh! Where was it?"

"I know where I'd *like* to meet him," Mr. Stanwood growled.

"You can't kid me, young fellow," Mr. Jenkins declared wisely. "My name ain't Jenkins. He! he! he! It's McMartin. Come along to the station, now."

Mr. Wilbur's hands closed, but his voice was like velvet.

"But we must go to New York, Mr. McMartin," he urged. "It's absolutely necessary. Will—will a hundred dollars be of any use to you?"

"No," said Mr. McMartin. "Come along."

"Two hundred?"

"Cut that out, and come along."

Mr. Wilbur was staring straight into his eyes.

"Is there no possible way to arrange it?" he inquired placidly.

"Come along, I tell you."

"Well, I've *got* to get to New York, Mr. McMartin," Mr. Wilbur purred. "I hate to do this, *but*—!"

And his right hand caught Mr. McMartin squarely upon the point of the jaw, whereupon the incorruptible one wrinkled up and went down like a lump of clay. Mr. Stanwood took one step forward.

"He isn't hurt," Mr. Wilbur explained calmly, as he daintily wiped his hands on a handkerchief. "He'll be all right in ten minutes. Now let's go to New York."

Mr. Stanwood gazed down upon the prostrate figure pensively. He wouldn't have believed that there was a policeman in the world who would have refused two hundred dollars.

"Well, it's done," he said philosophically. "Let's go."

They were just turning toward the automobile when a mounted policeman galloped past it, coming toward them.

"Now, we *are* in trouble," remarked Mr. Stanwood grimly. "If anything happens, Dan, you take the car and run for it. I'll be hanged if I'll let a couple of mudhead policemen stop us now. I'll see this thing through, by ginger, if it costs a million dollars."

"What's the matter here?" demanded the uniformed man as he dismounted. "Did your car hit him?"

Thirty years in Wall Street had fitted Mr. Stanwood to meet emergencies.

"No," he said, after a little pause. "A little personal difficulty—that's all. There's nothing serious the matter. It was only a knockout."

The mounted policeman satisfied himself as to Mr. McMartin's condition, then arose and faced them.

"Which one of you hit him?" he demanded.

Mr. Stanwood's hand closed warningly on Mr. Wilbur's arm.

"I hit him," he lied glibly. "I was walking along here alone; he was impertinent to me and I did that. This gentleman came up in his automobile a moment later and stopped to see what was the matter. He doesn't know anything at all about it."

A hint was as good as a mile to Mr. Wilbur. By Jove, this old chap knew *how* to rise to an occasion. The uniformed man stood staring mutely into Mr. Stanwood's face in the dim light, with a glint of recognition in his eyes.

"Seems to me I've seen your picture somewhere," he said at last. "In the Rogues' Gallery?"

"Oh, I dare say," remarked Mr. Stanwood. "It's in every other publication you pick up."

"What's your name?"

"John Smith, of course," he said cheerfully. "Come along. Don't stand here palavering all night." The officer turned to his restive horse an instant, and Mr. Stanwood spoke aside to Mr. Wilbur: "Now, Dan, it's up to you. If you fail to finish it I'll cowhide you. After it's all over, come back and get me out of hock."

XXII

M r. Wilbur and the mysterious veiled lady were skimming along toward Sixty-fifth Street and Susan; Mr. McMartin was lying on a couch in the back room of a police station counting a procession of star clusters, and Mr. Fulton Stanwood, knight-errant, with one criminal charge against him and a few others impending, sat contentedly on a bench in the captain's office in gentle meditation. He was a sacrifice upon the altar of adventure, and—and it was bully, that's all! Talk about jousting for a lady's glove! He only hoped Dan would be able to get through all right. If he didn't—if he didn't! Well, a fellow who didn't have enough gumption to carry away a simple adventure like this wasn't the man for *his* son-in-law!

Away down in Sixty-fifth Street, in the drawing-room of the Rev. Dr. Hawthorne, Lieutenant Paul Abercrombie Harwell Rowland sat phlegmatically watching Susan as she paced back and forth, pausing anxiously each time at the window to look out. Not a word from Dan Wilbur! Not a word from Marjorie! Not a word from Lieutenant Faulkner! Of course it was possible that Dan had been held up, or pursued, or something; he'd appear all right, and she could depend upon Marjorie's cleverness to keep her identity away from him. But suppose she hadn't? Suppose Dan had found out who she was, and had taken her back home? And where, *where* was Faulk? Suddenly Susan turned upon Paul.

"Oh, I'm *so* worried!" she announced. "I feel just like crying."

"Go ahead," he suggested considerately.

"I won't!" she stormed.

And then she pouted. Susan was irresistible when she pouted. Her lips looked like a rosebud, and tears of aggravation glistened in her eyes. If Dr. Hawthorne hadn't been in the next room, and the sliding doors hadn't been open, Paul would have—would have—but he was, and they were—so!

"Where can Faulk *be*?" she demanded for the twenty-ninth time.

"I haven't the faintest idea," Paul responded as usual.

"And the others?"

"Ditto."

"I know Faulk must have been hurt, or killed, or something, and there you sit like a dummy and let me do *all* the worrying."

"I don't know whether he has been or not," said Paul aggravatingly, "but I'll gamble that he gets here—dead or alive."

As a matter of fact, at just that psychological moment Lieutenant Faulkner was entering a telephone booth in a Forty-second Street hotel. Oddly enough, he had asked for the Stanwood residence in Fifth Avenue.

"Is Mr. Stanwood in?" he inquired calmly.

"No, sir," replied a man, evidently a servant.

"Or Miss Stanwood—his sister?"

"No, sir. They are both out, sir, and we don't know where they are or when they will be back."

"Well, will you please tell them when they return to come at once to the Rev. Dr. Hawthorne's home in Sixty-fifth Street?" and he gave the number.

"I doubt, sir, if they can come tonight," explained the servant. "Some important family affairs, sir, and—"

"Oh, yes, they'll come," the Lieutenant interrupted confidently. "You tell them that Lieutenant Faulkner—Lieutenant Robert E. Lee Faulkner—is waiting for them, and they'll *come* all right. Goodbye."

An automobile drew up in front of the police station and stopped with a blatant honk. Mr. Stanwood jumped. Great Scott! Had Dan been caught again? He peered anxiously out of the door of the captain's office to see who came in. It was a woman—a thin, angular, aristocratic looking woman.

"Elvira!" Mr. Stanwood almost shouted.

He forgot he was a favored prisoner, and rushed into the outer office. His sister turned, amazed, at the sound of her name.

"Well—Fulton!" she exclaimed.

"Go back in that room," commanded the desk sergeant harshly. "Any tricks like that and you'll go in a cell."

Mr. Stanwood meekly sneaked back into the captain's office, and stood peering out. His sister stopped nonplused. In a cell! Her brother! Fulton Stanwood! And did the man live who dared to order him about like that?

"I'm a prisoner, Elvira," Mr. Stanwood explained humbly. "I hit a policeman. What are you doing away up here?"

Miss Stanwood told him tersely. First, there was Marjorie's elopement with Lieutenant Faulkner, which came to her knowledge indirectly. Marjorie had confided in her maid, the maid had told a man servant, and the man servant informed her. Mr. Stanwood listened as if stunned. Then came a detailed description of the chase in the automobile from Central Park up St. Nicholas Avenue and through Tarrytown.

"Their car broke down within a couple of hundred yards of our place in Tarrytown," Miss Stanwood went on to say. "We had lost sight of them momentarily. They got another car somewhere, and were just leaving their broken-down car when we sighted them. They had picked up another man, too—some white-headed old idiot who'd lost his hat."

Mr. Stanwood gulped hard and was silent.

"Then they simply outran us," she continued. "Their car was the better. I've had everyone searching for you, and stopped here to telephone home to see if you had been home or had been found."

"But it wasn't *Faulkner* she eloped with," Mr. Stanwood corrected finally. "It was Dan Wilbur."

"Dan Wilbur? How do you know?"

"Oh, I *know* all right."

And then Mr. Stanwood told *his* story. She listened to the end without an interruption—an unusual thing for a woman to do—and then, severely:

"So it would appear that while I was in the rear car trying to stop them, you were in the front car giving them active assistance?"

"It would certainly appear so, Elvira," he acquiesced sadly.

"Well, don't you know your own daughter? Can't you see?"

"Oh, she had on all sorts of veils and things, and—and—besides, Elvira, I never heard of a man who had enough nerve to ask the father of the girl he's eloping with to help. And why *should* she elope with Dan Wilbur?"

Miss Stanwood was regarding him sternly. Mr. Stanwood dodged.

"Well, Fulton," she said in measured tones, "you are perhaps the most perfect specimen of an idiot I've ever met."

"I believe I am, Elvira."

Mr. Stanwood stood helplessly for a moment, then suddenly went out to the desk sergeant.

"I must go down town," he began authoritatively.

"Oh, you *must*, must you?" sneered the sergeant.

"But listen a moment, sergeant."

And really it was worth listening to. He pleaded and threatened and coaxed and raved and wheedled and swore. It was all the same. And finally he told him his real name—a magical password in three countries. The sergeant only smiled insolently. Then Mr. Stanwood blew up in one desperate effort.

"I didn't hit that confounded McMartin, anyway. Bring him out here and he'll tell you I didn't."

Mr. McMartin came out, fully conscious now.

"That ain't the fellow that hit me," he protested. "It was his chaffer. Where is *he*?"

"You see," remarked Mr. Stanwood loftily, "you have no charge against me."

"Oh, yes," Mr. McMartin broke in. "I charge you with being an accomplice before the fact and after the fact, and attempting bribery, and speeding an automobile, and threatening an officer, and profanity, and—and being a suspicious character. I guess them ought to hold you for a while."

"Why not add murder and arson and the rest of it?" Mr. Stanwood demanded savagely.

"Won't he take money?" asked Miss Stanwood timidly.

"Sergeant, how about a cash bond?" asked Mr. Stanwood.

The sergeant talked it over with Mr. McMartin, and finally decided that two thousand dollars would be about right.

"Very good," commented Mr. Stanwood. When anybody mentioned money he was in his element. He knew that his sister usually kept two or three thousand dollars in her desk at home for current expenses. "Elvira," he directed briskly, "'phone down, have a servant smash your desk and bring all the money they find there."

He was the first officer now, and she was only the crew. She went into the telephone booth, and a moment later came out frankly excited.

"Lieutenant Faulkner—" she began, "—Lieutenant Faulkner has just this minute left word at the house for you and me to come at once to Rev. Dr. Hawthorne's in Sixty-fifth Street."

Mr. Stanwood glared at her with lowering brows.

"Faulkner, eh?" he said coldly. "Of course *I* can't go." He glanced at the clock. "There is a suburban train down from the station over here in ten minutes. You get on that train, Elvira, go there, and if there's been no marriage—if it isn't too late—you see that there isn't until I get there."

Miss Stanwood caught the train, and fifteen minutes later took a cab from the Grand Central to the Sixty-fifth Street address. Just as her cab turned into the street from Central Park West, she saw an automobile draw up in front of Dr. Hawthorne's. She knew *that* car! A man assisted a veiled woman out, and they went up the steps together.

Miss Stanwood burst into the drawing-room, and everyone present, except Dr. Hawthorne, exclaimed, "Miss Stanwood!" with varying degrees of amazement and anxiety. There was Susan, clinging to Paul, and Mr. Wilbur with the oddest sort of an expression on his face, the veiled lady, and the mild, startled looking minister.

"I'll take charge of this young lady," Miss Stanwood declared authoritatively, and she did. "You'll come right into the study here, my dear, and remain here until your father arrives."

Susan turned with a broken-hearted whimper, and Paul gathered her in his arms protectingly. After all their trouble, too!

"Where *can* Faulk be?" she asked for the thirtieth time.

"I haven't the faintest idea," Paul responded as usual.

Miss Stanwood closed the door on her prisoner, then calmly drew forward a chair and sat down to wait. Mr. Wilbur stood staring at her. There were so many unanswered questions knocking about in his brain that it gave him a headache. He knew the elder Miss Stanwood. What did *she* have to do with it? Then came an awful thought. Gee whillikens! Was that Marjorie Stanwood—that veiled lady—and he'd helped her to elope? And had he not only helped her—his heart's desire—to elope with another man—but he'd made her father help? Oh! Oh-h! Oh-h-h-h! Then his eyes chanced to fall upon Susan in Paul's arms. He blushed for her utter shamelessness! That chap couldn't be the bridegroom—he acted more like Susan's husband. And where the deuce *was* Susan's husband?

There was a long tense pause, broken only by Susan's gurgling sobs; then, unexpectedly, Mr. Fulton Stanwood appeared before them in person, hatless and violent.

"Marjorie's in here," Miss Stanwood told him, quite as a matter of fact.

"I forbid the—the—this thing," Mr. Stanwood bellowed at them. "Where is he?" and then his eyes fell upon Mr. Wilbur. "So *you* did it, eh?" he went on coldly, insolently. "You wanted to pay your attentions to my daughter! I suppose that was merely a part of the trick?"

Mr. Wilbur colored slightly, but he was perfectly calm.

"I know nothing whatever about all this," he said deliberately. "I have acted in the best of faith throughout, and in this rather unfortunate—I may say utterly unexpected—development I proceeded blindly to help another man whose name, even, I don't know. I dare say," he went on impersonally, "he will be glad to speak for himself now."

Paul disengaged himself from Susan's clinging arms and stood forward.

"I'm responsible for all of this—so far," he said curtly. "Mr. Wilbur was in no way to blame for anything that has happened."

"Who the deuce *are* you, anyway?" Mr. Stanwood blazed.

"Lieutenant Rowland, U. S. A.," was the reply. "Lieutenant Paul Abercrombie Harwell Rowland."

Mr. Stanwood passed one hand across a bewildered brow.

"Were *you* going to marry her?" he inquired.

"Fortunately I am already married to the most charming woman in the world," replied Paul, and Susan shot a quick, imploring glance at Mr. Wilbur. "I was acting for another man."

"Faulkner, eh?"

"Lieutenant Faulkner, yes."

"Well, where is *he*?"

And just at that moment Lieutenant Faulkner stood in the doorway.

"*There* he is *now*!" exclaimed every person in the room in chorus.

"Hope I didn't keep you waiting," remarked the lieutenant cheerfully.

Mr. Stanwood turned upon him fiercely.

"Oh, it's you, is it?" he thundered. "You young—you—you—!"

Lieutenant Faulkner stood perfectly still, smiling.

"I'll ask that you don't express your opinion of me here," he said easily. "There's a minister present."

XXIII

Lieutenant Faulkner played the game according to the rules, trump for trump, so long as the rules seemed to adequately cover the particular conditions to which they were applied. But he was liable to introduce a dazzling variation at any moment; finesse a five-spot, for instance, while the other players looked on with their mouths open. Now there was a calm self-possession and cheerfulness about him that irritated Mr. Stanwood to a superlative degree, and at last:

"Well, Mr. Stanwood, what are you going to do about it?"

"Do about it?" raged Mr. Stanwood. "I'll never allow this marriage—that's one thing certain."

"Your daughter, I believe, is twenty-two years old and I am thirty," the lieutenant went on. "Just how would you prevent it?"

"I'd prevent it by—by—er—" and he hesitated. "I'd prevent it, by—er—I'd cut her off without a cent, sir."

Lieutenant Faulkner nodded.

"Very well," he said. "And then?"

"I'd disown her."

"And *then?*"

"I'd—I'd—," and suddenly Mr. Stanwood grew perfectly calm. "She shall choose between us, here and now. Open that door, Elvira, and let Marjorie come out."

"Now, just a moment please," Lieutenant Faulkner requested. "This may be the last opportunity I shall ever have to hold a conversation with you, and I wouldn't miss it for worlds. As I understand it, your only valid objection to me is that I haven't any money?"

"No, that is not all," and Mr. Stanwood glared belligerently into the young man's eyes. "I don't like your impertinence, I don't like your style, I don't like your methods."

"Just as you wouldn't like the methods of the man who defeated you in Wall Street, supposing such a thing possible," supplemented the lieutenant. "Well, say it is my lack of money, because it would be manifestly unfair to *you* to compare pedigrees. Now we don't care, either one of us, for your money. Do you understand that?"

Mr. Stanwood began to sputter and spout again.

"You may take it and build a bonfire with it," the lieutenant went on deliberately. "Kick your mansions into East River, sink your yacht, wreck your railroads, dig up your estates, burn your office buildings, light your pipe with your bonds, and melt up your gold reserve and feed it to the cat. It may surprise you to know that money isn't everything to everybody. I love your daughter—not your fortune—and she loves me. From the moment I knew she loved me you never had a chance; as I told you I asked you for her hand as a personal favor to you. Now I trust we understand each other; that's all I have to say."

There was a long, heart-breaking silence. Mr. Wilbur said not a word. He was a well-bred gentleman, trimmed to pattern, with the raw edges turned under and sewed. From a refuge in her husband's arms Susan taunted him with her eyes. Mr. Stanwood reluctantly admitted to himself that at last he had found one man whom neither mere money nor bluster would awe.

"Elvira, let Marjorie come out," he commanded.

And then Lieutenant Faulkner finessed his five-spot.

"She's not in there," he remarked, pleasantly. "She's waiting for me outside in an automobile. We were married two hours ago."

"Married? Already?" Mr. Stanwood blurted. The others echoed the exclamation.

"You see," Lieutenant Faulkner explained, "the elopement plans were, of necessity, made known to my—my *wife's* maid, and she betrayed us. I found it out just in time to send another maid along, heavily veiled, to fulfil those plans, and while that was being done Marjorie and I were married, for fear there would be an accident or something. I imagine that's the maid you have in that room."

And it was. Mr. Fulton Stanwood, knight-errant, gazed full into the eyes of his comrade in adventure, Mr. Wilbur, and they both blushed. And of course everything ended happily. Marjorie—Mrs. Lieutenant Robert E. Lee Faulkner—appeared before her father; and that man who can resist the mute appeal of soft brown eyes and the caress of round, white arms, and the quivering of red, rosebud lips, is no sort of a man at all. Mr. Stanwood *was* a man, a red-blooded, vital, human being. What *could* he do?

Half an hour passed.

"You folks had all better run over to the house with us and have a sort of wedding supper, I suppose," said Mr. Stanwood at last.

"Is that an invitation?" inquired Lieutenant Faulkner meaningly.

"Yes, confound it," said Mr. Stanwood shortly. "I suppose I'll have to have it engraved and send it to you by a liveried messenger?"

"Oh, that isn't necessary," and Lieutenant Faulkner laughed happily.

Mr. Wilbur met Susan at an afternoon tea.

"Silly blunder I made," he told her. "You know I thought all along that Faulkner chap was your husband?"

"Why, Dan Wilbur!" Susan exclaimed demurely. "Where *did* you get such an idea as that?"

"I don't know, you know," he confessed. "Stupid of me, wasn't it?"

And on her way home Susan paused to send a telegram to her aunt in Philadelphia:

"Everything is all right. Faulk won."

And, of course, she was to blame for it all.

The End

A Note About the Author

Jacques Futrelle (1875–1912) was an American journalist and mystery writer. Born in Georgia, he began working for the *Atlanta Journal* as a young sportswriter and later found employment with *The New York Herald*, the *Boston Post*, and the *Boston American*. In 1906, he left his career in journalism to focus on writing fiction, producing seven mystery and science fiction novels and a popular series of short stories featuring gifted sleuth Professor Augustus S. F. X. Van Dusen. In April 1912, at the end of a European vacation, he boarded the RMS *Titanic* with his wife Lily. Although a first-class passenger, he insisted that others, including his wife, board a lifeboat in his place. He is presumed to have died when the passenger ship sunk beneath the frigid Atlantic waves.

A Note from the Publisher

Spanning many genres, from non-fiction essays to literature classics to children's books and lyric poetry, Mint Edition books showcase the master works of our time in a modern new package. The text is freshly typeset, is clean and easy to read, and features a new note about the author in each volume. Many books also include exclusive new introductory material. Every book boasts a striking new cover, which makes it as appropriate for collecting as it is for gift giving. Mint Edition books are only printed when a reader orders them, so natural resources are not wasted. We're proud that our books are never manufactured in excess and exist only in the exact quantity they need to be read and enjoyed.

Discover more of your favorite classics with Bookfinity™.

- Track your reading with custom book lists.
- Get great book recommendations for your personalized Reader Type.
- Add reviews for your favorite books.
- AND MUCH MORE!

Visit **bookfinity.com** and take the fun Reader Type quiz to get started.

Enjoy our classic and modern companion pairings!

www.ingramcontent.com/pod-product-compliance
Lightning Source LLC
Chambersburg PA
CBHW020311150626
46552CB00022B/2713